AMERI⟨

by
R. J. Ross

America's Grandson
Cape High Book 2
Copyright © 2013 by R. J. Ross
All Rights Reserved

Dedicated to those that need love. AKA all of us.

CHAPTER ONE

My name is Trent Styles. I'm sixteen years old today, and the only visitor I've got at the moment is a white haired super hero called Firefly. No, she's not here to do the entertainment, before you ask, she's here to grill me again.

"So... he's not even mentioned me?" she asks, sitting on my desk chair backwards, resting her chin on her hands and pouting like a child. She's got to be somewhere around thirty--which you can't really tell. I figure she'll look like she does until she's well into her hundreds or something, I know Mastermental does. "Not a word? You're best friends with his kids, he should talk to you, right?"

"He hasn't said a word," I say, lounging on my bed and staring at my cell phone. I want to call Sunny. "And I'm best friends with Sunny, not Zoe. Max would kill me if I claimed his girlfriend as my best friend," I add, tapping on the screen to check my email instead. Maybe Sunny sent me something again. He still hasn't gotten a phone yet, but they've got a computer!

"But you go over there all the time, right? You're even coded into the security system," Liz says. Yeah, Firefly's name is Liz--Liz Masters. She's the half sister of Sunny's dad, an ex super villain called Technico. Technico got out of the Cape Cells a few weeks ago. The Cape Cells is a high level prison created by supers for supers. It specializes in keeping dangerous people with powers off of the streets. While Technico was stuck there it seems his girlfriend had twin kids, and almost two years ago she disappeared, leaving the twins in a foster home until Technico claimed them. Sunny's one of those kids.

Long story short, Liz wants to know about her brother. She hasn't seen him in fifteen years or so. My question is, though, "Why don't you just go talk to him? I really doubt he's going to jump down your throat or something."

She looks at me, and then looks down. "I can't," she says in a childish tone.

"Why can't you?" And stop wasting the first birthday I've had with actual friends, I add silently. I blink as I see I've got a new email, opening it with a slight grin. "Zoe killed the microwave," I read aloud. "That's a new one. Usually it's the TV," I add with a laugh.

"Did she really?" Liz asks, hopping off the chair and onto the bed next to me to steal my phone. "Man, I wish I could see that. Nico used to blow up all sorts of stuff when we were kids--it was hysterical."

"I bet if you go now you'll be able to see its remains," I tempt her. She gives me a dirty look and hands the phone over.

"Even if I could go over there, I couldn't get in," she says. "I took a look at the security system he's tossed up. It fried three pigeons and a gnat. He's really serious about keeping his new place safe, and knowing him, he's set it up against wiretripping." Wiretripping, as she calls it, is her traveling along the wire as electricity and exiting through a plug-in. She can get in anywhere, except, possibly, her brother's apartment building.

"It's 'cause Zoe was in the newspaper," I say. "He's paranoid because the twins are just now coming into their powers."

"You can get in, though!" she says. "So why don't I hook you up with a mic and a camcorder--"

"Do you want to come with me?" I say, ignoring her strange plotting. Liz tends to go about things in the most cockeyed manner you've ever seen. She will never say or do something straight forwardly. It's amazing that she can even be a hero with a personality like hers.

"I told you I can't!" she says.

"Then you can stay here," I say, pocketing my phone and heading for my door. She's up and behind me the second I take a step into the hall.

"You're going over there?"

"It's my birthday, I can probably talk Technico into making me something," I say shamelessly. Her arms wrap around me from behind--no, she's not hitting on me, don't go thinking strange things--and she flips over, suplexing me onto the floor and pinning me there like a wrestler.

"You can't go over there!" she tells me.

"Leggo."

"If you go over there Technico will ask about me and then--"

"Liz, honey, can you stop manhandling my son?" Mom says in an amused tone. I'm let go of, thankfully, as Liz hops to her feet and looks at her best friend--my Mom.

"He deserved it," Liz says, as if she hadn't just attacked me. "It's not fair going off to see my family without me!"

I'm not hurt. As the son of America's Son and Star Spangled, I'm pretty tough. My powers are simple enough, super toughness (almost invulnerable--not quite, but pretty up there,) strength, speed, agility, hearing, and I'm learning how to fly--but they're *extremely* super. Of the four of my group, I would probably be considered the tank. Needles break on me, getting hit with a Mack truck would break the truck before it broke me, and I'm pretty sure I could punch down a building if I tried. Sounds cool, sure, but it's not as cool as what the others do. Zoe's a technopath, Max's got gravity powers, and Sunny--Sunny's an elementalist. He controls plants and possibly the earth itself. In other words, I could be considered the boring one of the group. I still haven't told them what I can do, simply because of that. I think Max has a few clues, though. Max seems to know everything.

"Trent, take Liz with you," Mom says, jerking me back to the present.

"I would, but she tries to hurt me when I offer," I say, straightening my clothes and standing.

"Well then I'll bring her with us when we come later," Mom says.

"What?"

"You can't have a birthday party without your guests, can you? And since Nico's being paranoid about letting the kids out of his sight, I thought we'd bring the party to them," Mom says. Since when has she started calling Technico by his name? Has she even met him yet? It's probably Dad's fault. Dad's practically strong-armed Technico into being his friend, and in Mom's mind a friend of

Dad's is a friend of hers. I wonder if Technico realizes that.

"So we're going to throw a party over there?" I ask.

"Of course! I want to meet the twins!" she says. "I've got the cake baking and everything."

"Has anyone told them that?" I ask.

"Oh, I told your father when he went to work on the school this morning," she says. Whether she's heard back from him or not, I have no clue. I doubt it.

"I'm going to go tell the twins," I say, rather than delve into that. The moment I take another step, though, Liz has her arms wrapped around me.

"You can't go!" she protests.

"I swear I won't say a word about you, even if they torture me," I drawl. "You need to get the guts up to go see him yourself. He's your brother, right?"

"Yeah... but I went behind his back and joined the Hall," she says. "He'll never forgive me!"

"Oh, honey, Nico's a Hall member himself, now!" Mom says. "Didn't I tell you that?"

"He is?"

"Of course! He's going to be the new school's principal!"

She's literally bouncing I notice as I step to the tiny rock in front of the abandoned looking apartment building. The rock shoots up, revealing that it's the top of a highly advanced panel. I press my hand to the screen, and then tap on the "Talk" button that appears. Nico's face appears on the screen.

"Hey, um, Technico?" I say, feeling a bit awkward. "Can I bring a friend up?"

"Who?" he asks.

"Your sister?" Liz pushes me out of the way.

"Nico? Can I come in?" she asks, looking serious. "I want to meet my niece and nephew and--"

"Where the hell have you been?" Nico demands. "I've been

out for weeks! And you're already programmed into the system so just press your hand to the screen," he says. The screen goes blank and Liz stares at it for a second before pressing her hand to it. A line of code flashes across the screen. First my bio and then hers appears on the screen. Glowing footprints appear on the concrete in front of us, lighting the way into the apartment building. I make sure to step on them.

"Step on the--"

"Oh, I know," she says, already following me. "Nico tends to be a bit showy like this."

Don't go telling people I said this--norms don't need to know, but the stronger a super is the stranger they tend to be mentally. Nico and Liz's dad? He was Superior--a legend among heroes, and even though he's dead now he still gets movies made about him. So if they seem a bit strange in the head, well, that's probably why.

The door swings open and Sunny leans against the frame, holding a pop. "Dad says come on up," he says, taking a drink.

"You're Sunny?" Liz asks--then promptly drags the poor guy into a bear hug. I grab his pop before he drops it from flailing and take a drink.

"I'm going ahead!" I say cheerfully as he makes muffled sounds of distress. He's probably going to get revenge for this, I think as I finish off his drink, but he's got to fight off an overly touchy aunt right now. I'm safe for the moment. I knock once and the door swings open, revealing Technico.

"So? Where is she?"

"Downstairs squeezing your son to death," I say, not surprised as he heads past me and down the stairs. "He might survive!" I add. "Possibly!"

"You mean Firefly is here?" Zoe asks from where she's sitting on the couch. "I want to meet her!" she says, rushing past me and after her dad. That leaves me alo--

"You seriously brought Firefly over?" Max asks from the kitchen. He comes out with a pop in his hand. "Why?"

"Because she suplexed me," I say, heading for the fridge as well. Yes, it's impolite to raid strangers' fridges, but this isn't a strangers' fridge. I've spent most of the last week hanging out here whenever school gets out--until I have to go home for dinner, that is. I grab an Orange Fanta, knowing that Zoe got them only because I like them, and head into the front room, dropping down in front of the couch in my usual place. Is it awkward being alone with Max? He's a super villain, I'm a super hero in training--

He drops down on the couch and kicks his feet up into the chair behind my head. "So, when are you transferring?" he asks.

I'll get back to you on that awkward thing. "You sure you want me to?" I ask. "If I'm not there you get more time trying to talk the twins into becoming super villains."

"It's not a party without a tank," he says. I glance at him, since he just bluntly admitted that he knows what I am. "What? With America's Son as a dad and Star Spangled as a mom, what else could you be? Or are you a dud?"

"I'm a tank," I admit, shrugging my shoulders. "No super cool powers like gravity or anything, just good old fashioned power. Or at least I will be," I add. "Dad says I'm still pretty breakable."

"Maybe for him," Max drawls. "You're probably the one they'll send after me when we're older, aren't you?"

"Really hard to crush a tank," I agree. Then I look at him, knowing that we both realize I'm the most vulnerable I'm going to be right now. He probably could beat me, and I think we both realize it.

"I wonder if they've thought of that already," Max says. "I'm surprised we don't have adults panicking over me knowing you."

"Are you going to kill me?" I ask. "Right now's probably the best chance you're going to get."

"Why would I?" he asks. He doesn't bother pretending to be shocked, though. I appreciate that fact. "There are several reasons I'm going to keep you around," he goes on. "One, you're one of us. Two, you keep Sunny busy so I can flirt with his sister, and three-- don't you think the massive battles are going to be awesome? Man, I seriously can't wait until you're in the air! Have they set you up with a uniform yet?"

"You're looking forward to it?" I say blankly.

"Heck yeah," Max says. "We should practice the really dramatic stuff, you know, like where I try and crush you and you toss it off. I want to make sure I don't over-do the weight, at least not until you're older. Maybe we can get a special class when the school opens up properly. Have you figured out your name?"

I honestly didn't expect this reaction. Let me explain. Max? He's a super villain at seventeen--he's smart, sly, and extremely capable of being devious. Thing is, more often than not, I'm pretty sure he's an open book. It's sort of unsettling knowing that behind the mask of the guy that once held an entire super bowl for ransom is a guy that I'm slowly starting to consider a good friend. He treats the whole super hero/villain thing like a football game.

"No, I just don't want to be called America's Grandson," I say. "All I really want is to be able to play football, actually. I'm not even thinking huge battles and tights," I admit. "You know how much it sucks not being able to play sports when you're... me?" I ask, glancing at him.

He's looking at me curiously. "You're going to spend your entire life trying to knock other guys down," he says after a moment. "Stopping cars from going off cliffs, saving school buses from flipping, all the good stuff, and you're worried about a bunch of idiot norms in helmets?"

"I'm sixteen," I mutter, feeling like an idiot when it's put like that.

"You just need a girlfriend," Max says. "You can't have Zoe, so we'll just have to find you another super girl."

"How does it go from wanting to play football to needing a girlfriend?" I demand.

"You feel like running up against hard to move objects, right? Sounds exactly like a girlfriend to me."

"I really don't see why Zoe picked you."

"Jealous?" he asks with an evil grin. "I have some news you might find interesting, though," he says, pulling a folded up piece of paper out of his pocket. He hands it over, waiting for me to unfold it. "I haven't told the others just yet," he says as I look blankly at the picture. "That's our first non-group student. At least she will be."

I'm staring at a short haired, punk girl with blue streaks in her choppy red hair. She's wearing jean shorts, combat boots, and a camisole--one that shows she's as flat as a board and says "Bite Me" across the chest. She's--

"Cute, huh?" Max says. "She's a duplicator."

"A duplicator?" I repeat, feeling a bit shocked. "Where'd she get that from?" I ask.

"Mother was an illusionist, father was a creator type--both died in an earthquake over a year ago. She was taken in by other supers," Max says. "I didn't hear anything about it, that's how under wraps she was. Her parents were part of the Southern Branch. She's fourteen," he adds.

"Help," Sunny calls from the front door. I get up, heading for the poor guy who's leaning heavily against the door frame. "She almost killed me," he gasps pathetically. "You jerk."

"Hey, now, this isn't my fault," I say, trying not to laugh.

"I could feel my spine against my stomach," Sunny goes on, stumbling into the room. He stretches, twists, and grunts before heading for the couch to grab my half empty Fanta and finish it off.

"Hey, that's mine!" I protest, following him in. "So did you just leave them down there?" I ask as I drop down in front of him in my usual place. You might have noticed, I don't like couches--or much furniture, actually. It always feels like it'll break.

"Yeah. She got a hold of Zoe, so I ran," he says, and then grabs the picture I had let fall when getting up. "Who's this?"

"Cape High's future student," Max says smugly. "Cute, huh?"

"What's she do?" Sunny asks.

"She's a duplicator--what does she duplicate, anyway?" I ask Max.

"Right now? From what I can find, only herself for a few seconds. I've got no clue how much she'll be able to do when she's older," Max says. "Might be she can only tag team with herself for the rest of her life--but hey, it's still a useful power. I figured I'd pass you the picture and let you two decide what to do with it."

"Huh," Sunny says. "Wonder what she's like."

"Not a clue," Max admits.

"Oh, crap, I forgot," I say abruptly. "Dad and Mom are coming over soon. Think I should tell Technico?"

"Your mom?" Sunny asks.

"Yeah... ah... they want to throw me a birthday party."

"TRENT!" I hear Technico bellow from the ground floor of the apartment building, "WHY IS YOUR MOM CARRYING A THREE TIER CAKE?"

"Um... whoops," I say. "Too late, huh?"

Principal Matkins stares at the computer screen, a frown on his face. He's positive, now. He'd wondered, of course, and had almost been certain that the twins' father was the super villain Technico. Now he's positive. After all, the man just blew up several cell phones in the YouTube video. Unfortunately now that he is certain he had supers in his school, the supers are already gone. They'd been withdrawn the day after he'd met their father. They wouldn't be coming back.

"Ms. Fell, if you would?" he says as he steps out the door of his office. Ms. Fell looks up from a folder, a curious and slightly irritated look on her face as she nods and heads for him.

"Yes, Principal?" she asks.

"Do you have any information on the Rosenthorn twins' whereabouts?" he asks.

"Ah--I'll see what I can find."

"Do you know if they had any close friends here?" Principal Matkins asks.

"The boy--Max, but he's transferred as well. Oh, and one other... Trent Styles," she says.

"Tomorrow I'd like to see the Styles boy in my office, if I could."

"Of course, Principal Matkins."

"Happy happy birthday to you! Happy happy birthday to you! Happy happy birthday dear Tr-entt, happy birthday to you!"

For once in my life there's more than just Dad, Mom, and Liz singing the song. I feel a bit light headed as I look around the table at everyone there. Then I blow out the candles as gently as I can-- only the top layer of cake goes flying. Max catches it with his gravity powers, slowing it to a stop.

"Boy's got some lung power," Nico says with amusement. Liz is hanging on him--literally. She's tucked under his arm with her own wrapped around his waist tightly. I've seen her get clingy before, of course, usually with me or Mom, but this seems strange to me. Maybe it's because it's an adult male, even if it is her brother.

Liz, as far as I know, has never had a boyfriend. Or if she has, it wasn't for very long at all. Actually, until seeing her like this, I've never really even thought of her as a girl. She might be crazy, sure, but she's one of the most amazing supers I've ever met. Like I mentioned earlier, she can actually travel along electrical wires if she needs to, although she says it gives her a headache. She's... *beyond* being "female" to me, I guess. Okay, I'm not making much sense, sorry.

She's my aunt as far as everyone in the family (including me) is concerned. She's also one of the most powerful supers in the Hall, possibly the world. I guess it only makes sense that she has trouble finding a guy she can hang onto in such a girly fashion. Finding a guy that just leisurely drapes an arm over her shoulders like Technico does now might be even more impossible. But... I can't help but think that maybe she'd like one. You know, other than family.

Seriously, though, I have no ability as a matchmaker, so I'm just going to shove that thought aside. Mom is talking at a mile a minute as she cuts the cake and hands out huge pieces to everyone. Max looks at the pieces, looks at me, and hands the top tier over without a word. I can't help but grin at that as I grab a fork.

"Your kids are so cute!" Mom says. "Zoe, honey, you look exactly like--" then she stops, glancing at Technico and Sunny as if she knows she just made a massive faux pas.

"My mom, right?" Zoe says. "Did you know her, Mrs. Styles?" she asks.

"Oh call me Jeanie," Mom says. "And your mother and I worked together quite often! She was a wonderful hero--whenever there was a disaster, she would come running. Oh, she never did the little things, criminals, super villains--" she stops, looking at Technico, "I mean she never went out and arrested people. Lady Rose was a specialist. She did so much and saved so many lives... I..."

"Well, then, why don't we play some games or something?" Dad interrupts. I note he's stolen the second tier of the cake. I'm not surprised. "Nico, have you set up the roof yet?"

"Still working on it," Nico says, eating his own cake. He's not saying anything about Lady Rose. In fact it's almost like she was never mentioned by the bland expression on his face. "But the basketball hoop is up. Anyone want to play a few rounds?"

"I'm up for it!" I say. I can almost hear my Dad tell me that I can't, that someone might get hurt--I even look at him, but he's grinning.

"I'm in," Sunny says. Now technically I should worry, right? How strong is Sunny? Sure he's going to grow up to be pretty tough, but--

"I'm in," Dad says. Now I'm really worried. Sunny won't get hurt, will he?

"How about some two on two?" Nico asks. "Me and Sunny against you and Trent, Ken? Unless you want to play, Max?" he asks the other male.

"Nah, I'll play winner," Max says, standing closer to Zoe, who is--elbowing him, it looks like. "What?" he demands. "I'm not betting--actually, why not?" he says, digging out his cell phone and typing furiously. "I'm going to make a ton off of this."

"Keep it super channels, only," Nico tells Max.

"Don't you have something to give to Trent?" Zoe hisses. More likely she bought a present and is forcing Max to do the giving. That's what Mom does.

"I already gave him a present," Max says. "What he does with it is totally up to him."

Cheapskate.

"You gave him the card?" she asks.

"I--do I have to?" Max asks in a whisper, which isn't fooling anyone. But hey, gift! I walk over and hold out my hand with a shameless grin, watching as he scowls and digs in his pockets to pull out a small envelope. "Here. It was the best thing we could think of," he says, handing it over.

I pull it open, staring in amazement at the gift. "Oh YEAH, twenty buck gift card to Burger King!" I shout happily. "I know what I'm doing for lunch tomorrow!"

"You got him a gift card... to a fast food restaurant," I hear Nico say even as I'm staring happily at my gift.

"Tacky, isn't it?" Max says mournfully. "But he's a walking stomach."

"He looks happy to me," Zoe says, sounding quite satisfied. Really, it sucks that she picked Max. The girl can cook AND give great gifts!

"Zoe, seriously, if you ever get tired of Max, I'm free!" I tell her, putting the miraculous gift in my wallet and wondering if twenty burgers can be eaten in one hour--or do I want fries, too?

"You're doing it again," Max complains. "Quit hitting on my girlfriend."

"And since no one told me it was your sixteenth birthday," Nico says, "I got nothing, kid. But--for this and let's say two day's work on the school, I'll take you to the junkyard and let you pick out--" he looks over at my Dad. "Scooter? Motorcycle? Car?"

"Hmm... I think he can pick for himself," Dad says. "It's not like a wreck is going to kill him. What do you say, Jeanie?"

"He has to get his license, whatever it is," Mom says firmly.

"Awesome!" I say. "Can I skip school tomorrow?"

"No."

"Now for our present for you," Dad says. "We've been talking about this for a while--but we think it's about time you get the chance to go out on the field. We've arranged a meeting with the Hall's tailor--"

"Heck yeah!" Max cheers. "I'm finally getting a nemesis!"

The adults stare at him.

"Did you tell him?" I hear Dad ask Nico.

"Not a word, but I guess it's not too hard to figure out," Nico admits. "BUT!" he says, raising his hands. Max stops cheering, looking at him curiously. "Since you're both future students of Cape High, I'll be overseeing your dramatic battles. Double M already called me up over this one. There will be no dirty fighting, no weight over... let's say three times Earth's gravity--"

"Trent's a tank," Dad says.

"Really?" Nico asks. "I wondered. Okay, five times Earth's gravity, and keep the property damage to a minimum. And since Trent's still learning to fly, nothing above fifteen feet," he says to Max. "We'll start somewhere empty, like the razed mall off the highway, how's that sound?"

I hesitate. I wasn't really focused on getting out in the field, but... if it's fighting Max, doesn't that make it like a football game in some ways? Going head to head with Maximum, I think, a grin starting to pull at my lips. "It'll be fun," I say, grinning at Max.

"That's what I've been saying," Max tells me, grinning back. "Can he skip school tomorrow?" he asks my parents, even though I asked them not more than a few minutes before. "For special classes! And if it's during work hours less norms will be involved, right?"

"He's got to get his uniform first," Mom says. "My little baby is all grown up and fighting super villains," she wails, dragging me over to hug tightly. I might be taller than she is already, but she can hug so tight that I can't move.

"Mom, seriously," I mutter, flushing brightly, "it's just Max."

"Hey now, I've already got an established name," Max complains, "you should appreciate it."

"It will help you, too," Technico says to Max. "You've been caught on film saving the day a few times too many lately, we need to remind them that you're the bad guy."

"I had no choice," Max mutters darkly. "So what about that basketball game?"

"Oh, right," Dad says. "Rooftop?" he asks Nico.

"It's not getting any lighter out there," Nico agrees as he heads for the stairs. I feel a little light headed. I'm finally getting to play sports! That one of them happens to be a massive battle with a pal, well... like he said, it's not that different from football, right?

Emily can't help but stare at the yellow strips that surround the massive canyon. It's things like this that make her want to do the wrong thing every time, she admits as she reaches out and pokes the plastic. She wants to see what's in there so bad. This is where she's going to go to school, right?

"I would be careful, if I were you." Emily turns, looking up at the man in full uniform floating in the air overhead. "The new principal of the school has been installing the security lately," Mastermental says as he lands in front of her. "Although I understand your curiosity, since you'll be spending the next four years here."

"I don't like school," Emily says. "I'll run away soon enough."

"You know, it was quite difficult hunting you--the real you--down," Mastermental says mildly. "I've changed your papers to cover up what you were doing, even my own son thinks you were being fostered by another super family, but changing a few records will mean nothing if you go back to what you were doing."

"I didn't ask you to do that," she says, glaring at him.

"My question is, why did you let the doppelganger live the good life?" he asks. "Of course I can find out for myself, but I would rather hear it from your own mouth."

"Why does everyone just assume that living with that family was good?" she snaps, turning on him. "Just because they're supers doesn't mean they're good people, you know. They--" She stops herself, looking away again. It was dangerous, speaking of these things, even to Mastermental himself. "I want to see it," she says instead, pointing towards the canyon. "The school for freaks."

"The school for supers," Mastermental corrects. "Like you.

Unfortunately, I'm not coded into the system so I can't show it to you. Tomorrow, though, I'll introduce you to Technico, and he'll show you around. Until then, would you like to meet the family you'll be staying with?"

"Family?" Emily asks, feeling a bit panicked at the very word. "I don't think so--" she stutters slightly, taking a step back. "Like a foster home, right? I don't want--" She almost falls over as he reaches out, her worry flashing in her eyes even as he touches her forehead.

A man appears in her mind. He's tall, broad shouldered, square chinned, tough looking--but he's grinning widely and eating what looks to be an entire cake. It looks like he's at a party. A woman appears next, tall and smiling, her long blonde hair pulled up in a pony tail as she cuts another cake and hands out pieces. Then a third person shows up--a teenager, Emily realizes. He's tall, looks a lot like the man, and is jumping for joy over something. She looks closer at his face, searching for something--something sinister or dangerous.

"I won't lie to you," Mastermental says. "For some time, Trent was a bit frustrated being a super, much like you are now."

"Was?" Emily asks. "How do you know he isn't, still? I don't think I want to risk it--"

"He won't hurt you," Mastermental says. "I won't pretend to know what happened to you, child, but I will offer my help if you ask for it."

Can she trust him? She steps back, feeling uncomfortable with him placing images in her head. It's strange, disturbing, even. It doesn't hurt, or even feel intrusive which makes her even more wary. He drops his hand. "You will, of course," he goes on, "have to go to church on Sunday, school daily, and follow curfew laws. Ken is a preacher in his daily life."

She looks away, not saying that she doesn't trust religion any more than she trusts anything else. Most likely they will be even more condescending and judgmental than the family she'd stayed with before. They'll probably beat her with the bible.

"Fine," she lies, "I'll stay with this family." At least a part of her will.

"You," Mastermental says, "not your doppelganger. It's too dangerous for you to split yourself for that long, you know. At your age you should be more careful--"

"I said I'd do it, I'll do it," she snaps.

"If there are any problems--any conflicts of any sort--I want you to call me first," Mastermental says. "I'll find a different family to put you with. Had you been in my district I would have done so a long time ago," he admits. "But you are under my protection now, thanks to the school." There's a hint of satisfaction in his voice and she abruptly wonders just how many other kids he's getting with this school.

"Trying to make little Hall members?" she says.

"No, my dear, if you desire to be a super villain I will arrange for it, as well," Mastermental says. "As long as you continue to observe the basic rules of being a cape, that is." He looks up, turning and looking at a group walking past. "Ah, there they are," he says. "Come with me, Emily, your new family is right ahead."

She hesitates, and then steps forward. She can run at any time, after all. No one except for this man in front of her would possibly know the difference.

CHAPTER TWO

"He's a lot tougher than I thought he'd be," I say, grinning from ear to ear. The basketball game had been a blast. For such a shorty, Sunny could jump! He was fast, too. "Did you see that dunk?" I ask Dad.

"Yes, I saw the dunk--I'm surprised you did, since you were the one who was supposed to be guarding him," Dad drawls.

"He caught me off guard," I admit. "I mean, he could have asked to use me as a step stool before doing it." My parents start laughing, completely unsympathetic. Before I can say anything, though, Dad holds up a hand to stop us as Double M steps into view.

"Ken," Frank says. "Nice to see you. You as well, Jeanie. And I believe I have congratulations to offer to you, Trent?" he asks. "I'm looking forward to your joining our ranks." He holds out a hand to me and I step forward, taking it.

"It's nothing huge," I say a bit sheepishly, "just an arranged brawl with Max."

"Max is looking forward to it, I'm sure," Frank says with a slight smile.

"More than Trent is, I think," Mom admits, wrapping an arm around my waist with a proud look. "Oh, we left Liz with Nico--I think she's planning on moving in."

"So she's finally visited?" Frank asks. "Ah, forgive me, but this isn't a mere social meeting. I need to ask a favor of you. You have a guest room, correct?"

"Yes, of course," Mom says, looking a bit surprised. "Can I ask-_"

Frank steps to the right, revealing the girl from the picture. "This is Emily Dreyton. She'll be going to Cape High as soon as it's officially open. I believe that will be next week?"

"Should be," Dad says. "I take it we're going to be the foster family?"

"If you don't mind," Frank says. It's an order, pretty much, even I get that fact. Thing is, though, I was the one that mentioned signing up for something like this after I found out about Sunny and Zoe. It was barely a week ago, actually. Right after Zoe and Max had to deal with one of Zoe's ex-housemates from her foster home getting super powers somehow and almost dying because of them. It's dangerous for supers to be too close to norms, I figure.

Frank is looking at me. "You don't mind, do you, Trent?"

I look at Emily. She seems tiny to me, barely taller than five feet, skinny and delicate looking. She's cute, just like Max said, but she's glaring at me as if in challenge. Interesting, I think, that I'm the one being asked. I glance back at Dad, then at Mom, both who nod.

"I don't mind," I say, shoving my hands into my pockets. "I mean, after what happened with Zoe and Sunny, y'know? It's safer if she's in a super home--but do you mind?" I ask her. "I mean, it's kind of... I would have stuck a guy with a guy's family," I admit, looking at Frank, "not a girl. Not that I'm going to do anything, of course," I add quickly. "It's just... a little awkward."

"You have a point," Frank agrees, "but I'm afraid your family is the only one that's volunteered for this job," 'and the only one I feel will be able to deal with this one.' For a second I think that he's said that second sentence aloud, but I realize that no one else is responding to it as I glance around. I look at him, cocking my head slightly. 'She has a habit of running off and leaving a doppelganger in her place,' he goes on silently, even as he makes idle chat with my parents. I wonder if they can hear his explanation, but they aren't showing any reaction.

'Why?' I ask.

'As far as I can tell without reading her mind, her last foster family was abusive in some manner. And since there were only females around her age I can only assume it was them--or the parents. I will be looking into it, of course.'

'Why are you telling me this? Shouldn't you be telling my parents instead?' I ask.

'Oh, I'll tell them soon enough, but you're the one that will be spending the most time with her,' he says. 'Treat her gently, boy, or I'll deal with the problem myself.' That's a warning, and we both know it.

"I'll keep her safe, I promise," I promise, looking him straight in the eyes, "on my honor as a Liberty." I lift my hand in the air, the oath as serious as I can get. My parents look at me in surprise. Using the family's super name in a term like that is something I've been taught to do only in the most serious situations. It's something that's considered a binding oath as a super.

"Put a clause on that," Dad says.

"Until she no longer lives with me or my family," I add obediently, noticing the shocked look on Emily's face out of the corner of my eye.

"Good," Dad says, patting me on the shoulder. "You've got your promise, Frank. My son's word is as good as mine."

"And mine," Mom adds.

I... really hope I can hold up my promise.

Mom takes Emily to the guest room as soon as we get home and I look at my Dad. "Sorry," I say. "Seriously sorry--I know I shouldn't have--"

"No," he says. "You know our rules. Yes is yes, no is no, we don't swear by anything, but a promise is different, I think." He walks over to me, placing his hands on my shoulders and looking me in the eye. "I'm not sure what Frank told you, but if it was serious enough to make you bring out the family's honor, it's serious enough to promise to do."

"It is," I say. "She--even Frank doesn't know exactly what happened, but he thinks the last family she stayed with wasn't... good." I feel a bit lame for using that simplistic way of explaining it, but I can't come up with another way. "And since I'm a teenage guy that's staying under the same roof as her, well, I figure she needs that assurance. I don't know how seriously she'll take it, but I..." I shrug, looking down and feeling like a little kid all of a sudden. I'm almost six foot tall--I promise to get a lot taller, even, but this is serious stuff. Hero responsibility.

Yeah, I said it. I know a lot of norms probably don't think of it--we're harder to hurt, can fly, etcetera, so it's taken for granted that we do dangerous things. We're built for them. Thing is, it also takes a certain mindset to be a *good* hero. It takes the belief that someone else's safety and wellbeing is more important than your convenience. It takes a lot of stuff that I haven't been tested on, basically. I blink as Dad grabs my face and kisses me on the forehead.

"You're a good kid," he says. "I was worried there for a bit when you kept losing your temper, but you're turning out to be worthy of the name I've got planned."

"I will absolutely NOT become America's Grandson," I say quickly. "Never. I'll run off and join the circus before you try tossing that one on me, got it? That's got to be one of the stupidest names I've ever heard--"

He's laughing. Not just a little snicker, either, he's laughing so hard that tears are falling. "But it'd be so fitting!" he hoots, holding his stomach. "America's Son and America's Grandson working side by side--"

"Moooom!!" I shout, "Tell Dad I'm not becoming America's Grandson!"

"Tell him yourself!" she shouts back.

"I would but he's laughing too hard to hear me!"

"I'll see if they can fit it on the cape!" she yells.

"NO!" I yell. "I'm moving in with Sunny!"

"Not on a school night!"

"Then I'm moving in with Aunt Liz!"

"Okay!"

"Noooo, don't leave me," Dad says dramatically, wrapping his arms around my shoulders and putting all of his weight on me. I ignore it, dragging him along with me as I start digging through my closet. I stop, though, as I feel someone watching us, and turn to look at the stairs that lead into my room. Emily is there, crouching in the shadows and staring at us--but the moment she sees me looking back she disappears. "Huh," Dad says.

"She's a duplicator," I say silently. "She can be in two places at once."

"I see." He stands up straight, messing up my hair (which is hard because I keep it so short) and looking at me fondly. "You don't mind being tossed up against Max, do you?"

"I'm looking forward to it," I admit freely. "I figure neither of us will get seriously hurt and I'll finally be able to go head to head with someone other than you, Mom or Liz. But I think he's looking forward to it more than I am, actually. Max has this big spiel on teenage supers and how we need to step up to the plate already."

"Max was born with his gravity powers," Dad says. "He didn't have to wait until puberty. That's why he's so impatient."

"Dad... about flying--"

"It'll come," he says, "don't worry about it. Now you've got school in the morning, so get to bed already."

"Yeah," I say, changing into my pajamas and wondering if Emily is going to appear again without me noticing. That's a bit disconcerting, actually. I mean, yeah I'm a guy, but having someone that can spy on you at any moment? I'm not quite sure what to do, honestly. It's got nothing to do with gender, I guess.

I'm tugging a tank-top on (thankfully I've already got my boxers on) when she speaks. "I don't need a bodyguard, you know." I turn to see her standing in the middle of my room with that same defiant look from earlier. "I'm perfectly fine without your stupid little boy scout oath."

"Yeah?" I say, trying to look as if she hadn't just walked in on me half dressed. I drop down on my bed, feeling rather exposed, and cross my arms over my chest.

"I figure you just want to look good in front of the real supers," she says. "Well too bad, I'm not going to be your ticket into the big leagues, so stop trying to walk over me--"

"America's Son's son," I say. "I'm a walking tank, best friends with an elementalist and already lined up to be nemesis of Maximum. I don't need a babysitting job to get into the big leagues." Okay, that might have been too harsh, I admit. "Look, Emily, I don't know what happened in your past--I figure it's none of my business, but right now you're... I dunno, like my new little sister or something, right?"

"Your--your--" she looks as if I've slapped her, I realize. For a second she looks as if I've rejected her--but that doesn't make sense, right? I just invited her into the family-- "I don't need a big brother. You just stay out of my way," she tells me, storming over to poke me in the chest with that demand. "Don't get near me, don't try and play that whole 'we're a family now' crap, either. I've been down that road before. I'm just here until I can find someplace better, got it?"

I should be offended, but my mind gets stuck on something it claims is more important. "Is this the doppelganger?" I ask, staring at her finger. I can feel it. That means if it is the doppelganger, it's solid. I try listening more closely. I can hear a heartbeat, too.

"Wh--why should I tell you?" she demands, looking a bit red now. She jerks as my hand comes up, and then stares at it blankly, and cross-eyed, as I hold it under her nose.

"You're breathing," I say. "Solid, breathing, heartbeat--this isn't the doppelganger, is it," I say. "It's too good."

"It is," she tells me. "This is the doppelganger. So you'll never know which is the real me. I fooled my old foster family for weeks."

I'm staring at her, trying to find something that might tell me which is the real one and which is the fake. "How long?" I ask abruptly. "Can you keep the doppelganger around for an entire day?"

"I don't need to tell you that," she says.

"If this gets hurt, do you?"

"I don't need to tell you that, either," she says.

"How tough are you? Do you have super speed? Strength?" I ask, ignoring her attitude. "Special abilities other than the duplication thing?"

"I didn't come in here to be grilled by you!" she snaps. "I came here to tell you to stay away from me. I don't need you, I don't need your family, or even your stupid school! I'm perfectly fine on my own!"

I should be offended, I think again, watching her poke me over and over again. On some level I think I might be, but there's this look in her eyes--one that looks a lot like fear.

"Hey," I say abruptly, "it's bedtime, and I've got school tomorrow, so why don't you prove that you want nothing to do with me and go to your own room?"

"I--I don't have to do anything you tell me to!" she says. This time I catch it for sure. That's definitely a look of fear in her eyes. "Even if you threaten me!"

"I'm not going to threaten you, but I'm also not giving up my bed," I say, heading for the bathroom, "especially not to a doppelganger." I close the door behind me. I brush my teeth and wash my face, then step into an empty room. Looks like she left, after all.

Little sister? The very term irritates the crap out of her, Emily decides as she angrily changes into her pajamas. He was so high handed! Bragging about everything, making her out to be a weakling that needed his protection--little sister!!

Here she had been thinking he was a little cute--and he's pulling the little sister card!

She tosses the excess pillows across the room before flopping down on the bed angrily. Then she stops, her mind going straight to her foster sisters from the old home. They'd been so nice at the start, she thinks, falling back and staring at the ceiling. They'd offered her some of their clothes, treated her to ice cream, gave her privacy when she needed to cry, little things like that--but then they'd started demanding things from her. Any money she got, any friends she made, anything she might even consider hers was soon theirs. And when she finally stood up to them, they'd ganged up on her.

She was only just coming into her powers at the time. She had gone to bed beaten, hurting, but her natural healing powers rid her of any telltale marks long before she could tell the parents. She fought back the second time, but they were older, they had their super strength, and more importantly, there were two of them. It happened again... and again... until she was desperate enough to get away that she forced her doppelganger to be perfect. The doppelganger took her abuse, took her pain, and Emily? Emily slipped out the back door with a bag of clothes and twenty bucks stolen from the foster dad. She hadn't looked back. Even starving on a street corner or freezing in an alley, she hadn't looked back.

Then Mastermental showed up as she was picking through the trash, told her that she was no longer a ward of the Southern Branch, and brought her here. A new school, a new family, and all the old worries left from her old home. She rolls over, curling into a tiny ball under the blankets and sniffling pathetically. She just hopes that Trent had been as serious as he looked when he promised to keep her safe.

No, she thinks, she can't expect anything out of him. That will only get her hurt more when he betrays her.

But a tiny little voice in the back of her mind is whispering, "Wouldn't they just hate me if they ever saw him?" For the first time she falls asleep with a little grin on her lips, dreaming of how jealous the two would be.

★ ★ ★

Morning comes. I stare blankly at the alarm clock that's screaming at me, make a fist, and crush it before yawning.

"Trent! Did you kill another alarm clock?" Mom calls from the kitchen.

"It started it," I say, rolling out of bed and heading for the bathroom. There's something I'm forgetting... I'm not sure what, I realize as I take a quick shower and tug on a pair of shorts. I'll deal with the shirt later, I decide as my stomach grumbles. I'm starving.

Mom's at the stove when I get to the kitchen, cooking. She looks at me, waving her spatula. "Put a shirt on! We've got a guest!" she tells me.

"But I'm hungry," I say, scratching my stomach.

"Trent," she warns.

"Fine," I mutter, turning and heading back down to my

basement to dig up a shirt. The only one I can find, though, is the Firefly shirt that Liz gave me for my birthday. Actually I've gotten a Firefly shirt for my birthday every year since I was born, thanks to her. She's such an egotistical aunt. When I get back upstairs, Emily's sitting at the table.

That's what I forgot, huh? I shoot my mom a look of gratitude and head to the nearest chair at the table, which just happens to be straight across from Emily. "Morning," I say, just to see how she reacts.

She gives me a dirty look.

"When people say 'morning' you're supposed to say the same," I say, leaning on the table.

"Trent, behave yourself," Mom says.

"Yes, Mom," I say, leaning back in my chair. I catch a glance of a strange expression on Emily's face, that same hint of fear from the night before. It's gone too quick for me to read properly, but it has me frowning.

"Emily, honey, do you like bacon and eggs?" Mom asks.

"Yeah," she says quietly, looking at the table.

"Is this you or is it the doppelganger?" I ask almost silently. She looks at me.

"Why should I tell you?" she whispers just as silently. A plate is placed in front of me and I look up at my Mom.

"Behave yourself," she tells me. "Just because we've got a cute girl in the house doesn't mean you can tease her, got it?" Then she's back to the stove, getting another plate ready.

"I'm not teasing!" I protest. "She's got this trick--" Emily kicks me in the shin. Then, when I just look at her, she kicks me again. "That doesn't work," I tell her when it seems she's going to scoot closer to the table to try for a third time. "You're just going to hurt your toes."

"Shut it!" she hisses.

"You know Frank's going to tell them," I point out. "And it's not going to change anything if they know--so why not tell them?" I start eating rather than waiting for a reply, and finish off my plate full of food quickly. "Mom I'm going to get going," I say.

"Bye, honey," Mom says.

Soon, I tell myself as I tighten my shoestrings, I'll have a bike or a car to take to school--except sooner than that I'll probably be going to Cape High and no one will care. Oh well, I think as I stand, for now, running it is.

★ ★ ★

"So," Jeanie says as she drops down in the chair her son's just left. "Did you leave any broken hearts behind you?"

Emily chokes, staring at the woman in shock. "Wh--what?"

"Oh, sweetie, you're adorable! I'm sure plenty of boys have broken their hearts on you. Trent doesn't have a girlfriend, you know," she says conspiratorially. "Or there's Sunny! Sunny's a wonderful boy--he's Trent's best friend. In fact, he's the main reason Trent's so much happier now."

"Um... Mastermental said he was frustrated by being a super?" Emily offers, digging for more information. Why? She was planning on leaving soon, right? But so far the worst thing that has happened was Trent calling her a "little sister." "He didn't look very frustrated," she says.

"Oh..." Jeanie says, frowning slightly. "For a while there, Trent was the only super his age around. He wanted to play football, but Trent is a tank category super--it's inevitable, since both his father and I are the same. He can't play football with norms. He could all too easily hurt them--or be found out, you know? I feel a bit guilty," she admits. "When I was in high school I was a cheerleader. No one notices that a cheerleader is hard to knock down."

"Um... this is weird, but... are you and his dad like, second cousins or something?" Emily asks. "I mean you're both blond and-- "

Jeanie starts laughing. "Oh honey, no!" she says. "Of course not! Ken is from the Liberty line--he's the great, great, more greats, grandson of Liberty Bell. Liberty Bell was one of the forefathers of the first Justice Militia, which happened a very long time before the Hall. My family comes from Sweden."

"A Swedish hero," Emily says blankly.

"Well they didn't stay there for long," Jeanie replies. "Not much to do, after all."

Emily looks away, feeling her shoulders shake with her suppressed laughter at the image of a super just sitting around, bored. When she hears Ken laugh all the way from his room, she gives in, giggling. Jeanie smiles into her coffee cup without a word. It's only when Emily is merely grinning that she goes on. "But Trent, well, he became frustrated and introverted as time went by. It's very difficult going to school these days," she says quietly, "especially when there's no one there you can talk about your life with."

"Is Sunny still going to school with him?" Emily asks.

"No, I'm afraid he isn't. Right now Trent's the only super at that school--but next week when Cape High opens, we're transferring him over. He's bearing with it very well. Of course more often than not he's over at Sunny's as soon as school is over."

Emily nods, looking at her plate. She is starting to feel curious about this Sunny kid, honestly. She glances up as Trent's father comes into the room, wearing a T-shirt with the word "Technico" in a cheesy style print across the front.

"You seriously found one?" Jeanie says in surprise.

"I had to get it online," Ken says, "but I found it!"

"Technico is Sunny's father, Nico," Jeanie explains to Emily when she looks blank, "He used to be a super villain. He got out of the Cape Cells recently!"

"But--aren't you a hero?" Emily asks Ken. "Should you really be wearing a super villain's shirt?" She watches as Ken heads for the stove to make a plate with the rest of the food.

"Just because he used to be a super villain doesn't make him one now," Ken says. "Jeanie, I'm going to work on the school for a few hours--"

"Oh, I was planning on doing the rounds today," Jeanie says. "I know Ms. Hilson starts talking about running away from the home about this time. She's ninety years old, I'm amazed she can even find the front door of the place."

"I can meet you about noon? We'll head to St. Peter's and check on Ernest after lunch," Ken says.

"And Phil. He's back in for his knees," Jeanie says.

"Um... what, exactly, are you talking about?" Emily asks, looking back and forth as they spoke.

"Oh, sweetie, Mastermental didn't tell you?" Jeanie asks. "Ken's a preacher for a local church."

"Yeah... but isn't it just a cover? You know, for being a hero?" Emily asks. "Like being a news reporter just to know what needs fixed--"

Ken drops down next to her, a huge plate of bacon and eggs in front of him. "Not at all," he says as he starts to eat. "The hero-ing is more of a side job, actually, preaching is my true calling."

"But--" Emily starts out, trying to picture this man wearing a suit and pounding on a pulpit. It just doesn't add up. He looks and acts nothing like the preachers she's seen on television--she'd seen him do nothing but be goofy ever since she met him!

"Well... I'll put it this way," Ken says, looking at her with a grin, "my job is saving people, right? Well when I do it, it's for a moment, when God does it? Lasts for eternity. And I'm man enough to admit when someone can do my job better than I can. Hey, you want to work as a grunt doing construction work or do you want to go with Jeanie to the old folk's home?"

"I can't just stay here?" Emily asks.

"Oh, but the ladies are so much fun, sweetie! You'll enjoy it-- they've got so many stories," Jeanie says, standing, "and you're much less likely to break a nail."

There's no way to get out of it, Emily realizes. She's stuck.

I'm stuck sitting in the uncomfortable plastic chairs outside the principal's office, wondering if I shouldn't have skipped after all. I stretch my legs out in front of me, trying to get comfortable, only to have to shift again as a teacher almost trips over my legs. Man this is annoying. I'm missing my first class for this, too. I wonder what

Emily is doing--she's probably being dragged around by one of my parents. I wonder if she'll get to meet Mrs. Moll. Mrs. Moll is hysterical. She was once the moll of a gangster, and when he died, leaving her with two kids and no wedding ring, she went out, bought herself a ring and changed her last name officially.

Okay, I know you figure we only hang out with supers--and to a point you're right, but church members are... I dunno, family in a way. Dad does all sorts of things for them, and Mom helps. I grew up following them around as a kid, checking up on this guy, seeing how this lady is doing. A lot of their time is spent in hospitals and nursing homes. That's why, right now, I'll almost swear that Emily's being dragged off to meet Mrs. Moll, or possibly see Ernest Grover.

"Mr. Styles?"

No, Mr. Styles isn't one of the--wait, that was Ms. Fell, wasn't it? I glance up at the tiny woman. "Yeah?" I say.

"The principal will see you now," she says, motioning to the office door I'm supposed to go through. I get up, shoving my hands deep into my pockets and heading through the open door.

"Mr. Styles, good to see you," Principal Matkins says, putting a folder down on his desk and looking up at me. He's nothing much to look at, short guy, starting to go bald, but I guess it doesn't matter, right? "Please, take a seat."

I head for the chair in front of his desk, sitting down and waiting. Have they already put my transfer papers in? They should have, I think. I know the Hall was working on them--

There's someone else in the room. I turn quickly to find a tall woman in a pencil thin skirt and heels so high that she's as tall as my dad.

"I see you've noticed Ms. Born," Matkins says. "Don't mind her, she's merely here to observe." He picks up another file from the one he'd been looking at, opening it. "Mr. Styles, I've been informed that you were friends with the Rosenthorn twins?"

I'm not supposed to lie, but I really don't think this is a good thing to talk about. "I know them," I say blandly. "They used to go to school here." Both truths.

"Have you heard from them lately?" Matkins ask.

How lately is "lately"? Like today? Today counts as lately, right? "Not really." Haven't heard a thing--I doubt Sunny's anywhere near a computer or a phone at the moment to send me a text.

"It's just, I've been asking around and the school that they're transferring into--I don't know anyone that's ever heard of it," Matkins says.

I find myself drowning him out in my mind, my attention going back to the woman in the corner. She's a super. Yeah, when you grow up surrounded by them, even spend a bit of your childhood playing in the Hall, you get to recognize them. She's definitely got super powers. Thing is, though, if I know what she is, she definitely knows what I am. My problem? I have no idea who would win if we fight.

"Excuse me, Principal Matkins?" I say. "I'm feeling a bit sick--I think I ate something ba--" I jerk, making gagging noises and cover my mouth. "I gotta go--" I mutter, rushing out the door at a jog and out of the school at full speed. Will she follow me? I dare to glance back, but see no one, so I slow down, duck into a random store, and pull out my cell phone.

"Dad," I say, "I shoulda skipped."

"What happened?" Dad asks. I can hear rock music and construction work in the background, so he's working on the school. I can't stand still, so I start walking through the dollar store, making sure to check behind me once in a while.

"Principal called me to the office--he had a cape in there with him. Started asking me about the twins."

"A cape?" Dad asks. "Who?"

"That's the thing, I don't know," I say. "I've never seen her before, and I really think Frank would have told me if there was going to be a new super coming to my school. I faked being sick and ran for it, but I don't know if she's followed me."

"Where are you? I'll send someone to pick you up."

"Dollar Store on 89th," I say, pretending to look at something so I could check the entrance again. "I don't want to lead her to you and having someone pick me up might do just that."

"Do you see her?"

"No."

"How about heading to Deep Rivers? Your mom and Emily are there."

"Okay." I look around--see a fire exit, and head out, much to the frustration of the people working there. Times like these I wish I knew how to fly properly, I think as I race down the street and into the country. It takes longer dodging things on the land. I pull to a stop in front of a huge brick building, straighten my clothes and go in. The lady at the counter looks up with a hint of surprise on her face. "Trent!" she says. "I thought you were at school today--your mother just showed up with a cute little redheaded girl."

"Hey, yeah, do you know whose room they're in?" I ask, stepping up to the counter.

"I think they're with Mrs. Hash," she says. "They brought the most delicious cookies, by the way."

"Thanks," I say, heading down the hall to Mrs. Hash's room. I can hear my mom laughing all the way down the hall. I knock on the door twice as I peek in. "Mom? Can I talk to you for a moment?" I ask, waving faintly at Mrs. Hash and glancing at Emily, who's looking through pictures. Mom looks a bit worried as she stands up and heads for me.

"I'll be just a second," she tells the others before I tug her down the hall a bit to explain. Her expression gets more serious as the story develops. When I'm done she's already pulled out her cell phone and tapped a contact, bringing it up to her ear. "Hi, Frank," she says. "Can you send through the transfer papers for Trent now? No, just send it through. We're going to need a new place to stay, too. Yes. Just in case. Yes. We'll explain everything soon enough," she says.

"Moving?" I ask, shocked.

"They've got your address at the school, honey. We're going to have to move and put out word to the church that we'll be moving them, as well," she says. "Ahhh, and I was so fond of that building, too."

"Don't you think you're over--" I stop, and then shrug. "Fine, how's Emily doing?" I ask, looking suspiciously in the direction of Mrs. Hash's room. Who's to say that wasn't the doppelganger?

"She's uncomfortable still," Mom says almost silently. "I think she needs some counseling, honestly, but we have to get her to open up before we can get to that point. I'm so glad that Frank gave her to us."

"We should tell Dad we're moving," I say, changing the subject.

"Okay, I'll call him, why don't you go on in and say hi to Mrs. Hash?" she says, tapping on her smart phone again. I nod and head into the room, leaving her to explain things to Dad. Suddenly I'm worried that we'll be too far away from Kansas City to go to Cape High. That would suck.

"What's going on?" Emily asks as I come in.

"I'll tell you later," I say. "Hi, Mrs. Hash," I add to the elderly lady sitting in the wheelchair. "How are you feeling?"

"Much better after having such a handsome young man visit!" she says cheerfully. I should be used to being hit on by old ladies, but I feel heat creep up my neck as Emily looks at me. Awkward.

CHAPTER THREE

"While I admit, it'd be easiest to move you across country," Frank says a little while later, "with Trent and Emily still so new to their powers, I would prefer keeping them close to the school." We're sitting in Technico's front room. I'm sitting in my usual spot, right in front of Sunny, who's snoring again. Sunny can fall asleep at the drop of a hat, but since this is important stuff I jerk my head back slightly, hitting him in the thigh.

"Ow," he mutters. "Man your head is hard."

"Wake up, I might be moving," I mutter.

"That'd suck."

"You can't move them," Max says. "Trent and I have a battle coming up."

"Unfortunately, Ken put their actual address on Trent's records," Frank says darkly. "We've gone in and changed the official records, of course, but there's no knowing if they have it in paper form. We're sending people in tonight to remove any physical proof, but for a cape there is no such thing as being too cautious. So," he says, looking at Technico to finish his sentence.

"I'd like to extend my welcome to our new apartment tenants," Nico says with a sigh. "The second floor is in working condition, but will need some cleaning up. You can pick any of the apartments you want, they're all empty--in fact this entire building is. You can even open it up into a penthouse style if you want to do the work. I've been planning to expand into the apartment next door, myself."

"It's a bit dangerous, though, having so many young capes in the same building," Dad says, frowning. "With Emily, that'll make four in one place. Are we certain we want that?"

"It's either we spread them out into places with less of a security system," Nico says, "or we stick them into a highly secure area, surround them with full grown capes, and dare the enemy to come at us."

"I'm moving in," Liz says from where she's squeezed her way in between Zoe and Max (much to my amusement). "And other than my rounds and any large problem that requires me, I'm free to stay here as security, too. No one touches my nieces and nephews," she adds with a few sparks flying--literally. Max yelps as his shirt catches on fire.

"Liz!" he says. "This is a brand new shirt!"

"Oh, sorry," she says, not sounding very sorry at all.

"I don't have to stay here," Emily says. "I mean, I'm the intruder here, right? I barely know any of you, and it's going to be crowded enough as it is, right?"

"You're staying," Dad says in a firm tone. "No running off, got it?"

"But like you said, it's dangerous to have so many cape kids--"

"Emily," I say, "It's an entire apartment building. It should be big enough for two families. And I made a promise, right?" I'm ecstatic, I'm not going to lie. Living in the apartment? Awesome! I won't have to risk running across town every day, getting to the new school will be a breeze, and I don't have to worry about Zoe blowing up Sunny's computer. Besides, Sunny sucks at typing, and I swear he sometimes falls asleep while writing texts.

Huh... Emily's staring at me now. Did I say something wrong? She was probably just looking for an excuse to run again, I think looking at her closely. Is this the doppelganger? I glance at Frank, but he's not acting suspicious, so I can only assume it's the real her.

"What did you promise?" Sunny asks me.

"I'll tell you later," I say, suddenly feeling everyone other than my parents and Frank staring at me avidly.

"And why is she staring at me, now?" Sunny whispers silently.

"I have no clue," I whisper back just as silently, although honestly in a room full of supers it's sort of a waste.

"I have one more thing to mention, since I'm here," Frank says. "I'm not sure it's a good thing, honestly, but Emily, the daughters of your previous home are asking to be admitted into Cape High."

Emily's face turns white and she sways slightly, looking like she's going to faint. I can't help but want to get up, but before I work up the guts she's already calmed down--and looking resolute. Well... crap, I think. She's going to run.

"They live too far away to come here, right?" I say instead. "On top of that, they're part of the South Branch, which makes them out of our Hall's jurisdiction. Right?"

"Normally I would use that," Frank says. "But I've already brought in Emily and am planning on bringing in a few others from other branches. There's one in particular in the West Branch that I'm intent on getting--another orphan. If I claim that I can't take them because of their branch, I'll be shooting myself in the foot, to put it plainly." He's looking at Emily now, and I wonder if he's saying something to her telepathically. I also wonder if it will make any difference.

I glance at the people on the couch behind me, my eyes falling on Max, who's sitting next to Sunny and looking at the rather pale Emily. He has a thoughtful look on his face. "We don't have much to show them," he says abruptly. "A few empty buildings and a high tech security system."

"Emily--" I start out.

"They can come," Emily says. Yeah, that's the look of someone about to do something drastic, I think. "I won't mind at all." That smile is definitely fake, too. She might be able to make a perfect copy of herself, but she really sucks at hiding her emotions. I can't help but think, though, that I'm being seriously underestimated. A full grown cape chasing us down is one thing--two teenage girl capes is another. This time I'm the one doing the staring. She looks away.

"So I take it the two sisters are a problem from your old family," Nico says to Emily, "not the father or mother?"

"I don't need to tell you that," she says.

"Sure you do," Nico says. "I'm your principal. Who's going to vouch for Emily?" he asks, looking at us. "If we're going to deal with this problem I need to know it's worth it."

"I will," I say.

Frank is looking at Nico. "I would appreciate you not breaking the code to deal with teenage girls," he says mildly. "You're still on parole."

"I can deal with it," Max says. "Like Nico said, I've been seen as the good guy a few times too many lately."

"Don't!" Emily says, making us all turn to her. "You don't even know me, okay, so why are you all so intent on taking my side? I could be a liar or a thief or--or anything! You're all morons!" She shoots to her feet, storming for the door.

"Don't go out of the apartment building," Nico tells her. "You're not cleared to leave, it could be extremely painful."

I see her nod ever so slightly before she leaves the apartment. I can't help but stare at Nico. "You could have just made her stay," I say after a second.

"I'm getting too used to teenage girls storming off," Nico admits.

"I'll go talk to her," Mom says, getting up and following after Emily.

"So what was the promise?" Sunny demands, poking me in the back of my head.

"He promised to protect her," Frank says, "for as long as she lives with him or his family."

"That is totally cheating," Sunny says.

Nico looks at us. "I didn't realize you two were like that," he says.

"He's offering up promises and all sorts of stuff before I even get to talk to her!" Sunny says, poking me in the head again. "It's bad enough that he's half a foot taller than me, you know--man I'm never going to get a girlfriend!"

"Ooooh, that sort of cheating," Nico says.

"Yeah... wait, what did you think I meant?"

Max is snickering by this point, so I shoot him a dirty look. "Shut it," I say, feeling my neck turn red. Sunny might not have gotten what Nico was thinking, but I did. "I like girls!" I add a bit too loudly.

"What--" Sunny stops, and I can swear I hear his brain catch up. "My own father!" he yelps. Max is laughing out loud by this time so I elbow him.

"Ow."

"Well anyway," Nico says, changing the subject a bit too

blatantly. "What about that other one? The one coming from the West Branch? That'll be another chance--"

"It's a male," Frank says.

And Max starts dying from laughter. Jerk.

She wants to leave, Emily thinks, her hand already on the handle of the apartment building's front door. It's just that she gets the feeling that that black haired guy hadn't been lying about it being dangerous. She still remembers the strange footprint path that she'd had to follow to get inside--and it had changed with each person. That was definitely a bad sign.

"You don't need to run off," she hears Jeanie say from behind her. "Emily, honey, I think it's time we have a serious talk."

Emily looks at her, wondering why she feels the urge to burst into tears. It's so frustrating, she thinks, everyone keeps pretending to be nice and she doesn't know what to do--she blinks as arms wrap around her, tugging her into a hug. Absently she notices that Jeanie has much, much more chest than she probably ever will, and Emily is right at chest level on the older woman.

"Go ahead and cry, sweetie," she says softly. "Just let it all out."

"I--I am!" she says, a tear trickling down. "I'm a liar! And a thief! And--and I should never become a hero! Mom and Dad must ha--hate me!" she wails as the tears start to fall freely. Why? A part of her is stepping out of herself, watching as this pathetic display goes on--literally. Her doppelganger appears behind her, more out of instinct than anything else.

"I see," Jeanie says, looking at the doppelganger. "I think," Jeanie goes on, "that that is a very wonderful doppelganger, indeed. You have great talent, don't you?"

"We don't want to trust you," the doppelganger says. "Our last family was nice at first, but then they turned out to be nasty."

She isn't telling the doppelganger to say this, she realizes. The doppelganger is speaking for them both. She wants to protest, but it's hard to speak when you're sobbing your heart out. Instead she's being picked up and carried to the stairs like she's a child, where Jeanie sits down.

"I know," Jeanie says quietly, "that you feel alone. That both of you do. But sweetie, we won't hurt you. If you're afraid of Ken, or Trent--"

"It wasn't the father," the doppelganger says, "it was the daughters. They... they beat on me," she goes on, looking at Emily. Emily can feel her eyes on her. "While Emily starved in the streets. We--neither of us--were happy, or safe. This is the happiest she's been since before her parents died."

"Sh--shut up," Emily finally gets out. The doppelganger disappears. It's creepy, in a way, because she hadn't realized that the doppelganger was starting to think for itself until now. She should have, she realizes. She'd left the doppelganger to live her life for her, it had to make decisions when she wasn't paying attention, otherwise it would look strange.

"Oh, sweetie," Jeanie says, rubbing her back. "Your parents absolutely don't hate you. What you did, you did because you felt you had no choice. But right now you have a choice, Emily. You can choose to trust us. I know that your... those girls coming here is traumatic for you, but you aren't alone this time. Trent made a promise, right?"

Emily nods against Jeanie's chest, not looking up. "But lots of people don't do what they promise to do," she mutters. She sounds pathetically nasal. She hates that.

"Trent will do it," Jeanie says. "He's a lot like his father. But you know what? I don't think you *need* Trent to do it. In fact, I think it's high time I offer my assistance to the next generation-- starting with you and Zoe!"

"Wh--what?" Emily asks, looking up at Jeanie blankly.

"We're going to have some girl power training! If they're going to let the boys play, I see no reason that the girls can't too! And sweetie, once we get you and that doppelganger working together, I bet those two won't see what hit them," she adds with a wide smile.

Emily sniffles, hope starting to sneak into her expression. "Re--really?"

"I wouldn't agree if they were norms, of course," Jeanie says, "but supers! They should know better than to pick on a girl just coming into her powers! I'm tempted to go and talk to their parents, too! They need to know what little monsters they've raised and take responsibility!"

A little smile pulls at Emily's lips even as someone from the stairs steps into view. "I like this plan," the white haired female says. "Can I play, too?"

"Oh, I would say so," Jeanie says. "What do you think, sweetie?" she asks Emily.

Emily looks up at the tough looking white haired woman on the stairs. She's got muscles, she notices, and a sharp, wicked look on her face. "Yes, please."

We start cleaning up the apartment on the 14th floor. There's a lot of work, but with everyone working at full speed we get it clean rather quickly. I've got my own room, and along the way some of the assistants from the Hall brought out stuff from our home, so I get to work putting the room the way I like it. It includes several trips downstairs and out of the building (and on the glowing footsteps each time) to get everything up, but I manage.

Soon my new room looks a lot like my old one did--just smaller. "Hey Dad?" I say, sticking my head out, "can I get my own apartment? I got too much stuff!"

"We'll talk about that when you're older," Dad says. I shrug and turn back into my room, only to stop at the sight of Emily sitting on my bed, her knees drawn up to her chest.

"Can you fly already?" I ask. The only way she could have gotten in was through the window--oh. "You're the doppelganger, huh?" I say, heading to try and stick more things into the closet.

"Emily's putting her things in her room," the doppelganger says.

"But she sent you here, huh? What for, to tell me to leave her alone again?"

"She knows I'm summoned," she says. "But she didn't consciously send me here. When you promised--did you mean it?" she asks, looking at me imploringly.

"Yeah I meant it," I say, giving up on the closet and shoving things under the bed. I look up at her as I'm shoving the last bit under. "So wait, what do you mean consciously?"

She shrugs. "Sometimes I can say the things she wants to, but won't," she says. I get to my feet then blink as I realize someone's standing at my doorway. "Emily," the doppelganger says.

"What are you doing in here?" Emily demands, coming into my room and grabbing her doppelganger, "Get out."

"Hey, hey, don't fight with yourself," I say--trust me, I realize how strange it sounds. "You're fine. I'm done unpacking anyway." I drop down on the head of the bed, motioning for Emily to sit down as well. Is it weird that there are two girls that are actually the same girl sitting on my bed?

Er... I think I shouldn't think too deeply on that fact.

"Why are you so comfortable with this?" Emily demands as she sits down on the foot of the bed. The doppelganger scoots back so her back is against the wall and she can see both of us.

"With girls on my bed? Yeah, I probably shouldn't be," I say. "But as long as we keep the door open I figure we won't get in trouble, right?"

Emily and the doppelganger stare at me. "What exactly are you thinking?" they both ask in the same dark tone.

"Hey, nothing bad!" I say, holding up my hands. "It's just ah... rules. Hey... why's the doppelganger out, anyway?"

"We need to practice," they say. "Your mom said she's going to teach us to work together for girl power lessons." Then Emily gives her doppelganger a dirty look. "Although you didn't need to show up in his room," she complains.

"Tag team fighting?" I say, ignoring the hints of in-fighting. "Yeah, makes sense."

"And we're here to tell you that if you suddenly turn into a jerk we're going to beat you up," the doppelganger adds, looking fierce. "We aren't going to run again. We're not afraid of you!"

I try not to laugh, but looking serious as I nod is quite a strain. "Makes sense," I agree.

"And don't laugh, because we're serious," Emily says, looking downright... nope, that might be her scary face, but it's pretty cute, really. In fact I can't help but want to see her try to beat me. It'd be fun.

Actually... this is sort of dangerous, huh? No, not just the sitting on the bed--both Mom and Dad are no doubt listening to every word we say, much less anything else, but her looking so fierce as she tells me that she and her doppelganger will beat me up--it's making me sort of like her. Probably not smart, I know. I mean, for one, she's under my protection, for another she's got a lot of stuff she needs to work through, stuff that's more important to deal with than prospective boyfriend girlfriend stuff, and for a third... well, I already told her she was supposed to be like a little sister, right? I'm definitely not seeing that, even with the red and blue hair (our family tends to wear a lot of red, white and blue, okay?)

But... despite all that stuff? I'm pretty sure I'm starting to like her. Crap, and here I was planning on giving Sunny a chance. Sorry, Sunny.

Really, really sorry.

I don't think I'm going to play fair for this.

"My question is," Ken says that night, well after the kids stopped talking and went to their own rooms, "why did Principal Matkins have an unidentified, undeclared super in the school to begin with?"

"Maybe she was trying to get a job as a teacher? Or at least claiming to. I'm not sure," Jeanie says. She curls in closer to her husband's side, resting her head on his shoulder. "Frank said he's got a few extras working the late night shift to see if they catch sight of her... oh, honey, I... we could have lost him," she whispers.

"No. Trent might not be fully grown yet, but the majority of supers would have a hard time taking him out," Ken says. "He's getting tougher by the day, you know. In fact I'm certain he would have held his ground long enough for help to come in."

"He did the right thing, though," Jeanie says. "By running the norms weren't exposed to a cape fight. I just... she was in our schools," she says, her hands fisting for a second. "How many others has she found that way?"

"I don't know--the only thing I can think is that none of the identified children have been declared missing--"

"What about ones like Emily?" Jeanie asks. "Ken, she was abused by her last family. The daughters ganged up on her, and when she couldn't handle it any longer she left her doppelganger in her place and ran off on her own. Had something happened to her, no one might have known about it until it was too late--she's not a tank like Trent, I doubt she knows how to protect herself--" she takes a shuddering breath and a tear escapes her.

"That poor baby," Ken says quietly. "She's been opening up to you?" he asks.

"Yes, thankfully. Liz and I are going to start teaching her and Zoe self-defense, by the way. I really should tell Nico we're going to."

"I bet Liz already has."

"True. Ken..." Jeanie says, hesitating for a second, "I think we should adopt Emily."

"I don't think Trent would appreciate that one bit."

"But--he seems fond of her!"

"That's why he wouldn't appreciate it," Ken says. "Honey, Trent is a Liberty all the way to the souls of his feet, you know that, right?"

"Of course I do--he's so much like you."

"Well Liberty boys tend to like feisty females. Ones that knock you out even though you're a tank and it's the middle of a battle," Ken drawls teasingly. "Emily, even after all she's gone through, is showing signs of fight, and she's one of the few females with powers that are around his age. I'm not promising anything will happen, of course, but it's too early to go 'here you go, Trent, your new little sister.'"

"I see... you're right, of course. But, you know, I just wish she had gone to the parents," Jeanie says, "instead of running away."

"Do you want to meet the parents?" Ken asks. "There could be a very good reason she didn't feel confident in going to them."

"I know." She just doesn't want to picture supers so blind, Jeanie admits silently. "I don't know if I should meet them," she admits. "I don't want to do something I can't take back."

"I know," Ken says.

"And I don't want those sisters coming to the new school," Jeanie says. "Not after what they did to Emily."

"Unfortunately, they're super kids," Ken says. "Unless some of the other branches decide to start up schools of their own, we're the only one available. And the only reason Frank feels he can start the school now is because he has Nico."

"Why is that?" Jeanie asks. "We could have put together something--"

"Nico is more than just the owner of the land Frank wants to use," Ken says. "He has a family name, of course--he's a Superior, but unlike the rest of us, he wasn't trained by his father. He created both Liz's and his own training program when he was thirteen years old. Frank is betting that he'll be able to do it for all the kids. Better programs than the ones we've passed down over the years."

"But in the hearing he was pushing the 'regulation' thing," Jeanie says, remembering watching Nico at his parole hearing quite vividly. In fact, that was the very reason she was so open to Trent going to the new school. A man that can clearly love a woman after sixteen years of being separated was not a super villain to the core. When he had stood and shouted that Summer Rosenthorn was Lady Rose, "is Lady Rose" actually, she had known for sure.

"Oh, they will be. Each will be trained by their teachers on how to act as a proper super, but they'll also be taught to be the best they can be. Honestly I want to hear what Nico thinks Trent's training should be. I might learn something from it."

"I wonder what he'll do with Emily," Jeanie says. "She'll make an adorable daughter-in-law, don't you think?"

"I think you're looking a bit too far in the future, honey."

"I should fix her hair!"

"You're not paying attention anymore, are you?"

"I'm sorry," Mark says, groveling in front of the woman. "I can't find him. The address I have is an empty house--I'll keep searching--"

"No," Star says. "Don't bother. That boy, even if you didn't notice him, is one of the bigger names' children. I'm not sure which, but I have a few guesses. I am not looking for children with a name behind them." She drapes one long leg over the other, looking for all intents and purposes as if this is a social visit. "You see, he knew me for what I am. Now I'm having quite a bit of difficulty even staying near this area."

"I--I see--"

"No, I'm afraid you don't see, Matkins," she says. Her eyes start to glow and Mark tugs on his collar, feeling the room get hotter. "What you have done is jeopardizing my entire business. It's brought me to the attention of the heroes. ME." The room is starting to feel like a sauna and Mark desperately tugs his coat off, fumbling with his tie. "I do not appreciate being put in this position, Matkins. In all reality I should kill you, but that would be too quick."

Matkins takes a deep breath as the heat cools. He's covered in sweat and his heart is pounding against his chest. "I--I didn't--"

"You can come in now," Star says mildly. The door opens and a man steps in.

"Tech--Technico?" Matkins gasps out only to scream as the world starts to rip apart.

"Well," Frank says the next morning. We're back in Nico's

apartment, where I sit where I usually do--although, a bit surprisingly, Emily has decided to sit down just a few feet away from me. Last time she was closer to where my Mom sat on the chairs brought in from the dining table. "When my agents went to the school they were surprised to find a little... problem."

"What little problem?" Nico asks.

"The Principal was laid out on the floor, incoherent," Frank says bluntly. "They brought me in, but I'm afraid his mind is quite a mess. I did get a bit of information from him, though, but it doesn't make sense."

"Why's that?" Dad asks.

"Because his mind is telling me that the one who did it to him was Nico."

"What?" Nico demands. "I don't--no I CAN'T mess with people's minds! It's impossible, trust me, I would have done it had I been able to!" We stare at him for that one and he has the grace to look sheepish. "Not that badly, or anything, but if you've got a talent like that you should use it!" he says.

"I'll strike that from the records, shall I?" Frank says mildly. "But the problem is we have no true leads--"

"We do," Zoe says, making me glance over at her. "We have a lead. It's just... not much of one."

"What's the lead?" Frank asks.

"There's a man out there--he's a super. He looks exactly like my Dad, except where Dad's hair is black the man's hair is white, and where it's white, it's black. I ran into him once."

"I remember that," my dad says. "Nico, you were looking for him, right?"

"Yeah. But I've found absolutely nothing on him. It's like he doesn't even exist," Nico says darkly.

"Well, it seems he does," Frank says. "Until we have more of a lead I suggest you all stay either here or at the school--"

"I should be looking for him!" Nico says sharply. "If he is a Superior, I'm the one that needs to deal with him!"

"No. We need you here more," Frank says. "They're after the children, Nico. You, the four of you," he looks to my Dad, Mom, Liz and back to Nico, "are our greatest defense."

"What about the kids we haven't brought here?" Mom asks. "Who defends them?"

"Their families. Those that don't have families, well, I'm working as fast as I can." He looks at Emily. "I'm afraid that today is the day the daughters of that family come. It was arranged by the head of the South Branch. They're here for a quick tour of the school grounds, which, honestly, I feel it's time for all of you to have as well. Especially since Liz and Jeanie have volunteered to teach a class once a week."

"They have?" Nico asks blankly.

"I sent you a ledger of teachers," Frank says, "and an email yesterday. You did read it, didn't you?"

"Unfortunately Zoe killed the laptop," Nico says blandly, "again. But welcome to the staff, ladies, I hope you know more about grammar than I do."

"We're teaching girl power," Liz says from where she's raiding the fridge.

"So a fighting class?" Nico asks.

"Oh, there's MUCH more than just fighting to girl power," Mom says. "It's all about attitude!" Emily's bright red by this point, but Zoe looks enthusiastic.

"I want to take it!" Zoe exclaims. "Emily, you'll take it too, right? It's for girls only, right?"

"We were planning on it," Mom says.

"We do have normal teachers, don't we?" Nico asks Frank, glancing at his sister a bit pointedly. I look away, trying to keep from laughing, only to see a strange expression on Emily's face as she looks at--Max? Is she looking at Max? I glance at the couch, trying to follow her line of sight.

Seriously, don't tell me she's fallen for Max. Max hasn't even said anything! In fact he's writing in a notebook. I jerk as Emily scoots over quickly. Is she going to ask about Max?

"Hey," she says, tugging me down and cupping her hands around her mouth so she can whisper into my ear, "is Zoe really nice or is she just pretending?"

Oh. Well that makes more sense. I can't help but feel a bit relieved, actually. I turn, mimicking her cupped hand thing and whisper back, "She kills TVs and computers accidentally. And she's really mothering, sortta bossy, but not mean."

"Hey," Sunny says, "what are you two talking about?"

"You," I say.

"We are not," Emily says.

"You can ask me--I probably have better answers," Sunny says. Emily frowns at him.

"No I can't, you're probably biased."

"How can I say if I'm biased if I don't know the question?" Sunny asks.

"Okay," she says, standing up and cupping her hand around his ear. I watch his face for a second as she whispers--then grin as he snorts.

"Sure she is," he says. "She started using that freaking blow horn on me every morning and every time I try and take a nap on the job she does it again," he says, not bothering to whisper. "And she's constantly telling me to put on my seatbelt--"

"Are you guys talking about me?" Zoe demands.

"Yep," I say. Emily's as red as her hair now.

"What exactly are you telling her?" Zoe asks, looking like she's going to beat both of us.

"How mean you are," Sunny says cheerfully.

"I was--they were--uh--" Emily stutters, only to glare at me (hey, it's Sunny that let it out!) and kick me in the thigh. "Ow! I stubbed my toe on your stupid leg," she says accusingly.

"Well I keep trying to tell you," I say.

"Don't joke about stuff like that, you two!" Zoe says, getting up and looming over me and Sunny. "It's not funny. This is the first girl I've met my own age that might be my friend, you know!" Now she's the one turning bright red. Then she promptly sits down next to Max, who pats her on the back a few times.

"It's okay, it's okay," he says in a placating tone. "Breathe."

"I'm disowning both of you," she says, looking around him to glare at Sunny and me.

"This is totally your fault, you know," I point out to Sunny.

"Eh, she does that once a week or so," he says, waving it off, "more for Dad."

"It's true," Nico agrees. "She's constantly disowning us and then making sure we eat about five minutes later."

"I'm the only one in the family with common sense!" Zoe declares. "Dad would forget to eat entirely half the time, and live off of junk food the rest! And Sunny's brain doesn't kick in until nine," she adds.

I start laughing. "It's so true!"

Sunny slaps me on the back of my head. "I still haven't seen your brain kick in," he tells me.

"It's waiting for a special occasion," I say seriously. The entire room starts to laugh, even Emily smiles a little. It's broken the tenseness that came with Frank's announcements, thankfully. I look at Frank. "So when's the tour, anyway?"

"Noon," he says. "I expect you to lead it, Nico."

"Yeah, sure," Nico says. "Emily, you've got a doppelganger, right? I'm going to need both of your information, full bios, fingerprints, everything."

"Can't you just take mine? The doppelganger is exactly like me."

"Might be, but better safe than sorry,"

"You've got a doppelganger?" Zoe asks. "Can you make her do chores and stuff?"

"Um, yeah," Emily says a bit shyly.

"I would LOVE to have that."

"We can hire you a maid," Max says. "If you want we'll get her a wig to look like your hair!"

"Max?" Zoe says. "Shut up."

"What? It sounded like a perfectly decent idea to me," he mutters.

"What are you writing, anyway?" I ask Max, since it's pretty clear by now that his mind isn't really with us.

"A plot to get rid of Cinderella's wicked step sisters," Max says cheerfully.

"I'm not Cinderella!" Emily says. "And I can take care of this myself." But Zoe's looking at the paper curiously.

"How did you get so much information on them, anyway?" she asks abruptly. "Did you hack the Hall computers again?"

"I don't need to hack, I just go on Dad's computer," Max says. "It's downstairs."

"What are their powers?" I ask, reaching out to stop Emily from getting up.

"Basic enhanced strength and speed, they're C class, possibly B with training," Max says. "They're popular at their school, so I'm not sure why they want to come in the first place--unless..." he looks at Emily, "they're coming after you," he says finally.

"I don't know why," Emily mutters. "They hate me."

"Revenge is *always* a reason."

"What happened, exactly?" Zoe asks. "You can tell us."

"I--I fought back!" Emily says. "I fought them! Don't make me out to be an innocent victim, okay? I bit them, a lot. But it just kept happening, over and over again, and I got sick of it," she mutters, hugging her knees to her chest. "They never stopped. Even when I had nothing to give, they kept attacking me over stupid things." She looks around, looking at the entire room of people watching her.

"And I heal--I heal really quick," she goes on, "so I never had any evidence, but they did. They made me out to be the bad one, and their parents accepted it. You probably would have thought the same thing, if you were there."

"They sound like jerks," Zoe says.

"They sound jealous, to me," Mom says.

"Of what?" Emily asks. "When it first started I could barely summon my doppelganger. She disappeared every time someone distracted me. They were already faster and stronger than me."

"But I bet you're cuter," Mom says.

"She is," Max says, but it's in such a casual tone that it's like he's saying the weather is good. "Oh, but Zoe's cuter," he adds abruptly.

"You're biased," Zoe says dryly. "I'm your girlfriend. Besides, who cares about that? It's not a good enough reason to hurt someone!" She gets up abruptly, walks right over my legs and drops down next to Emily. "I think what we need to do, instead of just trying to get rid of them, is show them that Emily's got friends and they can't go after her anymore." She wraps an arm around Emily's waist. "Right?"

"I'd rather stick with the torture plot," Max says. "I have the designs all drawn up--they should be strong enough to hold a C class with no problem."

"Really Max, please restrain from mentioning those things when I'm in the room," Frank says dryly.

"Ah, right, sorry Dad," Max says. "I'll wait until you step out."

"I agree with Zoe," Mom says. "The best way to get rid of bullies is to stand up to them and show them they don't have any power over you anymore. Plus, fighting back doesn't seem to work--"

"It would if I did it," I say.

"Trent," Dad says.

"What? It would," I say. "I might not be as cool as the others, no special unique powers, or anything, but I have my purposes."

"It'd be overkill," Max says bluntly.

"I think you're very cool!" Mom says.

"Mom, seriously, it doesn't count when it comes from you," I mutter.

"Trent's not cool," Max says. "He's going to be the poster boy for Cape High, the guy that every aspiring hero wants to be like, he's more of a... prospective school legend--how do you not have an ego the size of a Mack truck, man?"

"Actually I thought I'd put you on the posters," Nico says. "It'd save me a lot of trouble and time, since only super villain wannabes will show up!"

"You're using Trent," Frank says. "We're bringing the tailor in tonight. The battle will go on tomorrow, closely watched, of course."

"Tomorrow?" Max asks.

"School opens officially on Monday. You're both going to be

our poster boys. Except I find that using the media is far faster than posting posters everywhere. So do make it nice and flashy."

Nico digs through his pockets, pulling out a handful of tiny metallic items which float in the air as soon as he opens his hand, forming into three tiny earbuds. "Here we go," he says. "These will work as three way walkie-talkies," he says, tossing one to Max and one to me. "That way we can plot it out."

"It's almost time," Frank says. "Shall we head to the school grounds? I'm almost positive that the sisters are waiting for us already."

"Do I have to go?" Emily asks in a tiny voice.

"You can do it," Zoe encourages her. She's still half hugging the other girl and I wonder why Emily hasn't shoved her off yet. Maybe Zoe's gotten to her, too. It's the mothering aspect, I think. Or maybe she has brain controlling powers that we don't know about. Or, I admit, it could have been how Zoe got so mad and started talking about being the only girl friend she might get. I can see that.

"Yeah," Emily says, standing. "But Trent has to pretend to be my boyfriend," she declares, pointing at me. "They won't realize he's a doofus with just a tour."

"What?" I say. "Uh, I mean--"

"I'll do it," Sunny offers.

"Oka--"

"She said me," I say quickly, grabbing her hand.

"Poster boy," Sunny mutters.

"Plant head," I say back. "Why aren't the twins the poster kids, anyway?" I ask as we head out of the apartment and down the stairs. I'm not about to let go of Emily's hand, I can already feel her trying to hang back.

"Because the average student will never become an elementalist," Frank says, "or a technopath, for that matter. You two are more... traditional, I suppose we could say. Also, neither of the twins have enough control of their powers to do a good showing."

"Basically he can't use them now, he can use us," Max says,

walking hand in hand down the stairs with Zoe--who is trying to maneuver closer to Emily. I can almost see what she's thinking, too, one to the left, one to the right, one behind and one in front. But it's not going to work if the sisters wind up coming here to school--

We're out the door. I have to let go of Emily's hand to take the steps through the defense field, but as soon as we step out of range I turn back, only to sigh at the sight of her going as slowly as she possibly can.

"Emily," I say. "Come on, let's get it over with. What happened to all that talk about girl power, huh?"

"If you go too slow the computer might get confused," Nico calls over his shoulder. That seems to affect her better than I do, and she comes out of the field a few seconds later.

"I was doing just fine," she says, flushing brightly. "I was coming, right? You don't gotta bully me over it."

"You were barely moving," I say. "Plus, Nico's still an ex super villain, I wouldn't put it past him to have the security program respond to little things like that." I grab her hand again, noticing how clammy it feels. "Do you want your doppelganger?" I ask.

"What?"

"If there are two of you to begin with, you're definitely going to be more intimidating, right?" I explain.

"I'd like to see it," Max says. "I've never heard of a duplicator cape except in history books once or twice. I wonder, actually, if you're as good as you seem at fourteen... there's a possibility of you becoming S class, isn't there? Or at least an A."

"Probably an A--simply because her strength and defense, while good, will never be great," Nico says from the front of the group. "Rapid healing is an amazing talent to have, but it doesn't beat not getting hurt in the first place. I'll be honest, of all of you, Trent is the most well rounded, I believe. I'll need to do a few tests to be certain, but--"

We're to the yellow tape that surrounds Death Canyon. In front of it stand two girls about my age, talking on cell phones.

"They're wearing high heels," Max says, sounding a bit incredulous, "and miniskirts. What do they think this is? A trip to the mall?"

I look at Emily then tug her closer, wrapping an arm around her waist and resting my hand on her hip. "Breathe," I whisper, leaning down slightly to say it. She's not looking at me, though, she's looking at the sisters--and she looks very, very angry.

This might not be a good thing.

CHAPTER FOUR

They smirked, Emily thinks as her hands tighten at her sides. They dared to smirk when they saw her! Of course those smirks faded the moment they saw Trent (yes, she's using him, she thinks, but he didn't protest too hard) and their expressions are now set in a look that she knew all too well.

We'll be taking that. She can almost hear them saying it aloud, she's heard it said so many times before. They just walk in, assuming that anything Emily has is theirs, ultimately, and there's nothing Emily can do about it--

I don't think so, Emily thinks so sharply that Mastermental turns and looks at her with a hint of surprise. He covers it up easily enough, approaching the two with a hand held out.

"Thank you for coming," he says mildly, shaking hands with Allie and Kelly. "I'm afraid that I personally have very little knowledge of the school building, so we'll have Nico lead the tour-- Nico," he says sharply, looking at the super villain who's in the middle of playing with the earbud he created for himself. Somehow between then and now it's become a full headset, complete with a screen. "Nico, if you would," Frank repeats sharply.

"Ah, right," Nico says, handing the strange machine to Sunny. "Hold onto this for me--and keep it away from your sister," he adds quietly. He steps to the front of the group, looking a bit bored. "My name is Nico Masters, my old cape name was Technico. I was recently released from the high security Cape Cells--"

"Wait, that means you're a super villain, right? Why are you leading the tour?" Allie asks.

"Because I'm the principal," Nico says, smirking slightly. "Make sure you pass that fact on to your parents. Now if we can continue," he drawls, snapping his fingers. The security system blinks into view. Lasers crisscross in a dome that covers the entire Death Canyon. A bird flies a little too close to the dome and one of the lasers turns, shooting it out of the air. "Usually these can't be seen. The lasers crisscross randomly, and shoot anything that goes within a ten foot radius of the dome without permission. This isn't all of the security measures, by the way, there are several I don't feel like showing you."

"Can I get one of those?" Max asks, looking at the dome in awe.

"No," Frank says flatly.

"Before entering the school yards I'm going to have to make some temporary passes for a few of you, and a permanent one for Emily, come here, kid," he says, motioning to Emily. She looks at him, wondering what exactly he's up to, then moves forward, slipping out of Trent's hold to stand in front of Nico. "And your doppelganger," he says. "If you plan on sleeping through my classes and sending her, I want to know."

Emily hesitates, looking at him for a moment, and then sighs. Her doppelganger appears next to her, and promptly turns to look at the sisters.

"Ditto," Nico says, snapping his fingers next to the doppelganger head. The doppelganger looks up at him. "Hand," he says, holding up a tablet for her to touch. The doppelganger, (who will be stuck with the name Ditto for the rest of her existence,) touches the tablet. Nico taps the tablet a few times, and then turns it, scanning Ditto with a green light. "Emily," he says, holding the tablet out to Emily and repeating the process. "By the way, I was right, a few major details are wrong--remind me to stick you in biology class, kid," he says to Emily after checking both stats.

"But the insides don't count!" she protests, flushing as Trent starts laughing. That doesn't bother her, but when the sisters start laughing derisively she feels her temper try to snap. Nico doesn't seem to notice as he taps on the tablet a few times.

"Sure they do, some supers have X-ray vision," Nico says, "or special tablets that can scan you. Now Double M, you're up," he says.

Emily and Ditto turn, their eyes going straight to Allie and Kelly. They're still snickering as if she's a moron for not getting her doppelganger's insides right. She takes a step forward, right in step with Ditto, their hands raised in fists--

Trent steps in front of them both.

★ ★ ★

Have you ever seen a petite redhead and a copy of herself look like they're about to launch? I'm seeing it just now, and it is--well, I'll be honest, just don't tell people I said this--it is freaking AWESOME. She looks like she's going to rip them a new one! She's looked at me somewhat like that once or twice, but this is a whole new level of P.O.'d.

"Trent," Emily snarls, "you're in my way."

"We're in public, Em," I say, wrapping an arm around Ditto's waist as she tries to go around me. "Behave yourself... yourselves."

"You laughed too," Ditto points out, and promptly punches me in the stomach. It almost hurts, I notice. "Ow," she says, looking at her hand. I start laughing again, earning a punch from Emily this time.

"She's so abusive," I hear Allie say.

"He was asking for it," I hear Zoe say in Emily's defense.

"Doesn't matter with him, anyway," Max says. Before Emily can lunge for the sisters again I grab them both in a group hug.

"Keep your head," I whisper to Emily silently. "Don't let them bait you. They're on your home turf this time."

She looks at me like she wants to argue, but something's stopping her. "Put me down."

"Will you behave?" I ask.

"Yes. But if they start something--"

"I've got your back," I promise. "Even though, seriously, you don't look like you'd need it," I add dryly as I look from her to Ditto before putting them both down.

"You--the brunette on the right," I hear Nico say. I turn to look at him as one of the sisters moves forward hesitantly. "My right," he says, motioning to the other one.

"I'm Kelly," she says.

"That's good," he says. "Touch the screen."

"What all are you learning from this?" she asks. "I mean, can you tell things about our abilities or something?"

"A bit," he says. "If you decide to come to this school I'll do more than just a quick scan."

"So you'll know everything about our powers?" she asks. "Like, that ranking thing?"

"Yeah, I'll know your ranking--and your prospective ranking," Nico says. "Hand," he adds, holding up the tablet for her to touch. She hesitates. "If you don't want the tour you can stand out here," he adds.

She touches the tablet, gets scanned, and Nico motions her sister to come forward. Max moves to Nico's side, glancing at the tablet. "Hey! He has no right to see those things!" the first girl snaps.

"I want to see Emily's," Max says. "Can you go back a few pages or something?"

"Max," I say warningly.

"Hey, can I see Trent's, instead?" Max asks. "C'mon, you didn't have to turn it off!" he protests as the tablet is put away.

"This is classified information," Nico says. "Meaning I don't give it out to the super villains they'll be up against later on... like tomorrow," he drawls. "Now, Star Spangled--"

"Oh, call me Jeanie!" Mom says, heading forward. "I'm certain you'll keep this information to yourself, won't you, Nico," she adds.

"Won't breathe a word," Nico promises, repeating the process. Then he moves to the left, revealing another highly advanced looking panel like the one at the apartment building. "Proceed in an orderly fashion, touch the panel, follow the footprints as usual, do not step anywhere OTHER than the footprints, and keep up with me--Zoe, start singing."

"Wait, what?" I ask, completely confused by why Zoe needs to sing.

"If she's focused on something else she's less likely to blow up my toys," Nico says as Zoe starts singing a--oh man--

"Justin?" Max asks. "Seriously?"

"It's the only one I could think of!" Zoe says before launching into the chorus. We pass through the security system, listening to Zoe singing off-key, and step onto the large platform that's built on the edge of the canyon. There are steps built into the side of the rock wall, leading down to the bottom of the canyon. Nico moves to stand in front of the steps.

"You can stop, kiddo," he says. "Ladies and gentlemen, welcome to Cape High. Our specialties will be hand to hand combat, ability training, and typical high school classes--provided by the teachers Double M's already set up."

I tug Emily and Ditto to the edge of the platform, looking at the massive campus built below. There are three buildings, each at least four stories high, and a huge metal field to the side. "What's that?" I ask Nico.

"A multi-purpose sports and battle arena," Nico says. "It can be changed to fit the occasion. If you get enough brawlers in the school I can even set it up for football."

"Seriously?" I ask, feeling like a kid at Christmas.

"Absolutely," Dad says. "I helped him design it."

"Now, if we can proceed," Nico says, starting down the steps. "School days will be longer than the typical high school, considering that we'll take an extra hour for abilities training. For some it could be even longer than that. Trent, Max, you're going to be working as mentors for the less experienced students--"

"I could use a mentor," I hear one of the sisters say. I glance back at her, seeing that she and her sister have moved closer to me. "I want to be the best that I can be."

"You'd need to be someone else to be that," Emily mutters.

"What did you just say? Because I seriously can't believe you just said that!" the girl says. "That was rude!"

"Yeah, it was really rude!" the other girl says. What are their names again? Lollie? Sallie? "We come all the way out here just to see you and you're like that?"

"I thought you came to see the school," Sunny says.

"Well we wanted to see our little foster sister, too," the first girl says. "We were worried about her, right, Allie?"

"She can't do anything on her own," Allie agrees. "She needs constant guidance--otherwise she winds up in situations she shouldn't be in."

"I'll show you a situation I shouldn't be in," Emily and Ditto snarl, trying to climb over me since they can't get free of me.

"Whoops, no you don't," I say, holding tighter. "I'm trying to go down steps here, Em, if you throw off my balance we'll all go down. It'd hurt. You, mostly, but it'd hurt."

"Then let me go!" Emily says, still squirming.

"Emily, sweetie," Mom says from ahead of us. "Please?"

They go limp and Ditto disappears, leaving me only holding Emily. "I can walk myself," she says.

"I don't mind," I say, but I put her down in front of me anyways, taking her hand instead. She glances at me.

"So... are you two dating or something?" Allie asks. "Because it just doesn't... fit. I mean, I get the goth couple--they're kind of cute together, but you and the football jock? You definitely don't suit him."

"Goth couple?" I hear Zoe mutter.

"You can write dramatic poetry for me later," Max says.

"I do not write poetry--dramatic or not!" Zoe says. "And where do you get off deciding who makes a good couple or not? It's got nothing to do with you!" I hear a popping sound from Allie's purse. Then I hear a popping sound from my pocket.

"Zoe, calm down, you just killed my transmitter," I say, pulling the sparking machine out of my pocket before it catches my pants on fire.

"My phone!" Allie yelps, digging it out of her purse. "You killed my phone! You little--" she lunges for Zoe, only to find Max standing in front of her.

"Do you know who I am?" Max asks as Allie stops.

"You're the boyfriend of the girl that just killed my phone!"

"Exactly," Max says, lifting a hand in the air.

"MAX!" I yell. "Can we get to the ground before you start a war? These steps might be tough, but I don't want to test it!"

Emily's shoulders are shaking. I look at her curiously as I hear the hints of laughter. "Hey," I say, poking her. The laughter escapes her, and she's giggling as we step off the final step.

"I don't see what's funny," I hear the other sister--Kelly,

maybe? say. "That was her phone!"

"That was almost her life," Emily says, looking back at them. "That's Maximum."

"Ma--Maximum?" she says. "The guy with the buses and the--"

"But he's so... short," Allie says.

"Why do people keep thinking height has anything to do with powers?" Max complains. Zoe hugs his arm, patting his forearm consolingly.

"You're still seriously cute," she tells him.

"Thank you."

I ignore it, focusing on Emily. She's got an actual smile on her face, I think, as if she's forgotten her enemies are right behind her. "So the idea of him crushing her cheers you up?" I ask her.

"Who wouldn't it cheer up?" she asks.

"Are you going super villain when you're older?"

"Maybe. It might be interesting."

I shake my head, sighing.

"This is absolutely not fair," Kelly whispers to her sister, hanging several feet behind the rest of the group. "She winds up in the Central Hall without even trying, and now she's got a boyfriend like that--it's absolutely not fair."

"Be patient," Allie whispers back. "Revenge takes work, right?"

"But I don't want to come to this stupid school!" Kelly says. "The principal is a super villain, it's in the middle of nowhere, and there are only three guys--one who's already threatened you, one that's stupid enough to actually date that brat and a third that is--" she looks over at Sunny, "short."

"But cute," Allie says.

"That doesn't matter. What matters is getting revenge," Kelly snarls silently, her eyes on the redhead. "Ever since Mastermental talked to our parents we've been on complete lockdown. No boys, no parties, nothing. It's all her fault."

"Then why aren't we doing something to--" Allie starts out, only to stop as her eyes fall on the thin man in question. Mastermental is so far out of their league that she's shocked at herself for thinking that. Even his seventeen year old son--who is her age--is way more than she and Kelly can handle--but-- "Her boyfriend," she whispers, looking at the tall blonde teenager. "Didn't they say something about him fighting Max?"

"I don't know, I wasn't paying attention!"

"But if he is--that means he's tough, right? So we need to make sure we catch her away from him," Allie hisses.

"Better yet, we need to take him away from her," Kelly says. "She's short, flat and totally lacking in sex appeal, right? So it should be easy, right?"

"That means splitting up. You go after him," Allie says. "I'll take on Emily."

"Not yet," Kelly says, "but soon."

"Make it quick, otherwise the tour will be over and we'll be sent back home," Allie says.

"I know that."

★ ★ ★

"This will be one of the classrooms," Nico says a bit later, leading the crowd through the first building. "For the most part this entire building is dedicated to classrooms like this one."

"And what's in the next building?" Frank asks curiously. I glance over at him, questioningly. "There was only one building planned in the original."

"We decided there should be more," Max says. "I built most of the second building. It's dedicated to the mad science and experiment training."

"And you let him," Frank says to Nico dryly.

"I like how the kid thinks," Nico says shamelessly. "You see it can work both ways--we'll train the super villains how to build things and train the super heroes how to break them down. There's even a special section dedicated to proper demolition methods.

That way it's easier to destroy buildings during fights without killing the norms as you do it."

"That... makes sense, actually," Frank says.

"That's insane!" one of the sisters says. "Why do any of it? It's like this is some sort of game to you!"

Frank and Nico look at her with bland expressions, their stances the same. "Really, child, you sound as if you're a norm," Frank says. "This is how we work."

"Honestly, I'd rather they didn't destroy anything at all," Nico says, "since I'm still going to be stuck on janitor duty after school is officially open. But if they swing too hard or such, well, it happens. Let's go check it out."

I follow along with the crowd, lacing my fingers through Emily's more to keep her from going after the sisters than to look like boyfriend and girlfriend. But she's looking all around as if trying to memorize everything. "Hey," she says abruptly, "you're going to destroy things tomorrow, right?"

"It's an empty lot," I say. "We might make a few craters or something, but I'm not planning on doing anything too stupid."

"I can bring in the buses, right?" Max asks, making me glance back. "I like to think they make for a good trademark."

"If you pay to get it replaced after you wreck it," Frank calls over his shoulder.

"Seems a bit extensive," Max complains.

"Maybe you can find something in a junkyard?" Zoe offers. "That's where we got the family car."

"Can you make it look like it works?" Max asks her.

"No."

"Oh, come on, you can try at least, right? It's got to be impressive!"

"Does no one care that I'm going to be hit with a bus?" I ask.

Emily looks up at me. "Not at all. I think your head is hard enough," she says with a grin before slipping from my hold. "Jeanie! Where's our class going to take place?" she asks, running to catch up with my Mom. Before I can protest, Zoe's following after her, leaving me walking with Max.

"Do you really mind the bus?" Max asks.

"Nah, should be fine," I admit. "But she just goes 'not at all,'" I complain. "You'd think she'd have a bit more fake compassion than that!" Max starts to laugh. "What? At least pretend to worry," I mutter, pouting. Yes, I'm pouting. My fake girlfriend should show fake compassion, right?

"You can take a hit with a bus, right?" Max says.

"Well, yeah, I figure. I'd hope, at least. Dad said I should be fine for heavy hits last time we sparred."

"I'll make it light the first time," Max promises. "So," he goes on, lowering his voice to almost silence. "How's it going with her?"

"I... have no clue," I admit.

"Well if nothing happens, tell me," Sunny says, blatantly joining the silent conversation as he catches up to us. "If the choice is her or the two sisters, well, I know who I'd pick."

"Seriously, Sunny, don't worry about it," Max says, dropping an arm over Sunny's shoulders. "You're an elementalist and your sister's seriously hot. You'll have your pick of girls and women as soon as you get a little older."

"What does my sister have to do with any of this?" Sunny asks darkly.

"Well I can't say if a guy is hot or not, you know? But you're twins, and look enough alike that if your sister is cute to me, you're probably cute to girls, right?"

"Maybe a girl just like Max!" I say. I swear we all picture it. Sunny literally shudders.

"No thanks," he says.

"Yeah, that might be a bit too disturbing," I admit.

"I get the feeling you're both mocking me right now," Max says.

"We are," Sunny and I agree.

"Jerks," Max mutters, giving us a dirty look which is a bit ruined by the twitch of his lips as he fights a grin. "Now, how do we want to deal with the sisters?" he asks silently. I glance back at the two trailing along behind the rest of us, a slight frown on my face.

"My question is why they even came," Sunny says. "They fit in with norms, don't seem interested in training at all--"

"Sunny, are *you* interested?" I ask him.

"I'd like to walk through the park at least once in my life without getting tripped," Sunny says. "And lately I've noticed that the rocks try to move if I stand still too long."

"Stand still," Max and I tell him in perfect tandem.

Sunny looks at us. "Fine, over here," he says, moving to the side of the path and standing completely still. For a moment nothing happens. Then Max points to the right. I look over, watching as a small pebble starts to vibrate against the ground, moving towards Sunny.

Yeah, it's just a pebble. Don't get me wrong, I'm sure there are plenty of supers out there that can make pebbles move--I know Max can make a lot more than just that move, but what you're not seeing is that Sunny's an elementalist. A plant elementalist--at least that's what we assumed. But there are no plants in Death Canyon. Everything was wiped out by Nico's weapon of mass destruction a while back, then what few weeds were trying to grow were wiped out by Frank's workers. This is all dirt, rock, and concrete.

That means Sunny might be able to control rocks or earth instead of just plants. I look at Max, Max looks at me. "You thinking what I'm thinking?" I ask.

"Yeah. Maybe." He looks at Sunny. "Sunny... you need to tell us now, which side do you plan on joining?"

"Huh?" Sunny asks. He's been distracted, I can tell, because he's looking straight up with his eyes closed, enjoying the sun.

"Are you going hero or villain?" I ask.

"Oh, that," Sunny says, looking at us. "Hero... in a way. Dad says I'll be needed for the big things, like forest fires or whatever. I've been thinking about it, and it sounds like a good choice. I mean, that's what Mom did, right?" he asks.

"So you won't be in the brawling game," Max says, breathing out a sigh of relief. "Good, wouldn't want to have to fight my future brother-in-law--"

"Hey, she's only fifteen, don't go planning the wedding just yet," Sunny says darkly. "But that should mean I can skip the brawling classes!"

"Don't even think about it!" Nico yells over his shoulder. "You're doing the full nine yards, boy!"

"Darn it," Sunny says.

"More than just having to fight your future brother, don't you think," I comment to Max quietly as Sunny goes back to sunbathing.

"Heck yeah," Max admits. "Sunny, you're going to be terrifying."

Sunny looks up with a sheepish grin, scratching the back of his head. "Nah, not really," he says. "I can't do anything yet, and Zoe still blows up everything that's got a circuit. We're slow learners, I guess. Who knows what'll happen?"

I suddenly realize that I've got no idea where Emily is. I glance over, letting out a sigh of relief as I see her chatting with Liz, only to frown as I realize something abruptly. "She's being way too calm about them being here," I say silently.

"Huh?" Max asks, glancing over. "Maybe she's ignoring it?"

"Emily's not the type to ignore something like this. She threatened to beat me up just last night if I even think of being a jerk," I say. "She won't ignore two people that she knows are jerks alread--"

I hear a scream from behind me. I already know what to expect as I turn.

Timing is everything, Emily thinks as she hangs on Liz's arm with a bright smile. She had waited until the boys were busy doing something and the adults were fully occupied, and the scream that comes from behind her is almost as satisfying as seeing the sisters try to cover up the fact that their miniskirts are slit completely down the back thanks to Ditto.

Ditto poofs out of existence just as the girls see her. Nobody else sees her, Emily notes with satisfaction, trying to look concerned and not gloating as she looks back to see what's happening.

"Nice," Liz says almost silently. "*Very nice*, both excellent timing and a believable alibi."

Emily gives her an innocent look, or tries to at least. Her eyes are gleaming with triumph.

"She slit our skirts!" Allie bellows, pointing at Emily. "That stupid thing she does--" she squeaks as her skirt starts to fall again, tugging it around her waist as much as she can. The skirt's too tight for it to overlap and give her a hint of modesty. "We're going home," she announces through gritted teeth.

"I'm afraid I can't allow that," Frank says mildly. "You see we've had reports of an unknown super in the area, we can't let young supers such as yourself wander around unaccompanied."

"Besides, you can't get out of the security dome," Nico says, completely unsympathetically. "Of course, Emily, you're going to have to be punished for that one," he adds.

"They could be lying!" Emily protests. "Maybe their fat butts were too big for the skirts and they ripped under the strain!"

Nico looks at her thoughtfully for a moment. "I'm willing to buy it!" he says cheerfully.

"Nico," Ken says with a hint of warning, "since Emily is ours and school isn't officially open yet, we'll deal with this."

"Are you all forgetting something?" Kelly demands. "We can't move! She totally destroyed our clothes! How are we going to continue this stu--this tour when we've got no pants?"

"I didn't do anything!" Emily protests, sounding perfectly honest.

"Ditto, huh?" Ken says.

Emily looks at him, feeling guilty all of a sudden. He'd called her "ours" she thinks. But she isn't theirs, right? She's just staying with them for a little bit-- "I'm not sorry," she says.

"We can't stay like this! Give us her clothes or something, she can run around in her underwear!" Kelly says. "She deserves it!"

"Max, go find them some duct tape," Nico says.

"Yes sir," Max says, racing off. He comes back a second later with a roll of black duct tape, tossing it at the sisters. Emily barely notices, because Ken is standing in front of her with a rather sad look on his face. The guilt, she thinks. The guilt--*it burns*.

"Emily," he says. She looks down, but he nudges her chin, forcing her to look up again. "Did you have Ditto slit their skirts?"

"I--they--yes," she admits, caught by those gentle blue eyes. A super hero shouldn't have eyes that gentle when he catches someone doing something bad. "You probably want me to move to a different home or something, right?"

"Oh sweetie--" Jeanie starts out. Ken raises a hand, stopping her.

"Do you think that's a good punishment?" Ken asks.

"Kick her out on the streets!" Allie says. "She'll never be a super hero! She'll probably become a super villain! She's nothing but lies--even her abilities are lies!"

"If you don't shut up, it'll be more than just your smartphones getting taken out," Zoe says, stepping in front of the sisters.

"Zoe," Trent says softly. Emily looks up at him, feeling betrayed by that one. "Step down," he says. "They're the ones that were assaulted this time."

"That's right," Allie says. "Emily's a wild animal--she's got no right to--"

Emily takes a step back.

"I'll apologize now," Trent says.

Emily runs, racing away blindly as the sound of Trent apologizing for her echoes in her ears.

CHAPTER FIVE

I reach up with one hand and flick her chest with one finger. I try and make it as light as I can, but the brunette goes flying several feet, hitting a wall. "But you don't talk about Emily that way," I finish, dusting my hands off. "Not when you're the ones that made her that way."

"Trent!" Mom says in a tone that says "even though I knew that might happen, I'm still not happy with you."

"How dare you attack her like that? She's a girl!" the other one demands.

"How about you? How about all those times you two ganged up on Emily when she was living with you? Do you really think we didn't hear you whispering earlier about getting revenge? Dad, you can punish me," I say, looking at my dad, "but I made a promise when this all started--"

The one that I flicked has managed to get to her feet and races towards me, slamming into me as hard as she can. I fall back, not because it hurts but because I wasn't expecting it. Instinctively I grab her, starting to suplex her like Liz does me, but she's grabbed out of my arms before I manage.

"No you don't," Frank says with a sigh. "She's barely a C class, Trent," he adds, putting her on her feet. The skirt is gone entirely, revealing a pair of black silk panties. I fall on my back, looking up at Frank rather than the panties girl. "You're already well on your way to A class. This would count as murder."

"I didn't--I wasn't going to--" I flush. "Right," I say. "Sorry."

"You're grounded," Dad says. "Now go find Emily. The moment you apologized she ran off."

"And you just let her?" I demand, hopping to my feet.

"She went that way," Liz offers, pointing to her left.

"Don't forget to tell her she has to help me cook for the next month!" Mom calls as I start off at a jog.

"That's her punishment?" I hear Max ask.

"Do you think it's too harsh?" Mom asks in a worried tone.

"Probably not," I hear Nico drawl. I wish I could fly right about now. If I could search for her by air this would be a lot easier. Then again, with so many people that can fly behind me, why am I the only one looking for her, anyways? I glance back at them, but even Zoe is just standing there--it's like they figure this is my problem to deal with, I guess. It probably is.

"Emily," I say. "Where are you?"

There's no sound. She's being perfectly silent, which is pretty impressive--no, wait, that's not a good thing when I'm the one stuck as "it" in this game of hide and seek! I let out a breath of air, heading into the second building. "You know, I probably shouldn't have done what I did," I say, shoving my hands into my pockets. "But you got off a lot lighter than I did, if it makes you feel better."

A tiny sound, almost small enough to make me wonder if it's my imagination, comes from the stairway that leads to the second floor. I head for it. "I know you hear me," I say, looking around the stairway wall and seeing the redhead sitting there. "So why aren't you answering?" I ask her.

She's been crying. She sniffles now that she's found, looking at me with a pathetic expression. "You--you apologized for me," she accused me. "You jerk! You tried to be nice to--"

"I didn't apologize for you," I said. I'm a bit surprised--had she stopped listening after that? "I apologized for what I did right after that," I explain.

"Wh--what did you do?" she asks.

"I flicked her," I said. "Sent her flying a bit--I tried to be gentle," I admit. "I'm grounded, by the way," I say, dropping down on the stair below her and leaning against the wall. "But I don't think they'll cancel the fight tomorrow, I'll just have to go home straight after," I say.

"You sent her flying?" she asks, looking shocked.

"Sure I did. I believe you when you said they ganged up on you, they're mean," I say. "I mean, you might be a bit wild, I gotta admit it, so maybe you do need apologized for--but not to the likes of them," I say, even as she kicks my leg. I grab her ankle, grinning as she tries to get her foot back. "You aren't going to run off on us, are you?" I ask.

"I want to," she says. "Your dad made me feel so guilty," she complains.

"He's good at that," I admit. "The first time I shoved a kid in school I got that look--the one that says 'I'm so disappointed in you.' It's worse than being spanked when it comes from him," I say.

"But they deserved it," Emily says. "Did you hear them scream?"

I fight a grin, shaking my head and looking up at her. "You know," I say, "you don't need to play dirty like that anymore."

"It's what I'm built for," she says, tugging her leg back again, trying to get free of me. I don't let her. "I'm not strong like you, I'm better at being sneaky."

"Yeah, but that'd be really useful," I say, stretching out across the stair and holding her foot hostage rather than give it back. It's tiny, I think, even her skull patterned canvas tennis shoes are small enough to be considered cute. "I mean, I'm not exactly built for stealth, myself. I'm going to be as big as my dad, or bigger. Having a friend that can pop in on super villains to listen in on their plots before disappearing again, it'd be handy. You don't have to be a super villain, even if you are sneaky," I tell her.

What? I just think it'd be a pain in the neck trying to get a date with a super villain. There's a reason that you don't see many couples like that--sure, Nico and Sunny's mom were one, but Sunny's mom was like Sunny. She was a specialist. Me, I'd like something like what my parents have. A tag team set-up. Sure they're both tanks and specialize in things like stopping runaway buses and traffic accidents and national disasters, but if we worked at it, I'm pretty sure Emily and I could figure something out--

I might be getting ahead of myself. Slightly. Just a little bit. I mean, she barely tolerates me still, right?

Well, I just need to work harder, I figure.

There's this moment, Emily thinks, where you can't listen to what's being said because you're so absolutely focused on one thing. This would be that moment. He's just lying there, stretched out and lazy, with her foot held captive--and all she can think of is Max calling her "Cinderella" before this.

If there was a more prince-like guy than Trent, she admits silently, she really doesn't think she'd survive meeting him. It's not even that fake kind of prince-like. At least she's pretty sure it isn't. He is definitely, absolutely, positively, not doing it on purpose, she figures. He's just too stupid to realize that he's making her crush on him.

Nooo, no no no, this is definitely not a good idea, she thinks. "Gimme my foot back," she says, tugging a third time. "You have no idea where it's been." He grins, and then laughs out loud, sending her poor heart pounding and making her hands feel clammy. "What if people come in?" she demands when he doesn't let go. "It looks like I'm stepping on you!"

"Nah," he says. "This is the easiest way to keep you from running."

"How do you know I'm not Ditto?" she asks.

"I can feel your blood pumping," he says, running a finger over her ankle. She barely restrains from shivering. "Hey, what super name do you plan on taking?" he asks. "It's got to be something interesting..."

"What about you?" Emily asks, wanting him to get distracted enough to let go. "You've got a name picked out, right?"

"I've got one I don't want," he says. "I'm absolutely not going to be America's Grandson."

"He's going to be Kid Liberty," Ken says, stepping into view at the bottom of the stairs. "Now up, we're heading upstairs for the tour." Emily finds her foot released and Trent on his feet before she can even realize what just happened.

"Kid Liberty?" he asks. "Not bad. I can live with that."

"Until you're older, then it might be just Liberty," Ken says, reaching down and pulling Emily to her feet. "Have you calmed down yet?" he asks quietly.

"I'm sorry," she whispers. "I shouldn't have done it."

"Because you feel guilty?"

"Because it doesn't make you and your family look good," she says honestly. "You and Jeanie have been so nice and I was--I'm sorry," she says again. "I don't want to--to go back or something."

He smiles and reaches up, messing up her hair. "We need to talk, but not here," he says. "Now up the stairs, we're blocking the way."

"Did they get their skirts fixed?" Emily asks. Only a part of her is thinking she doesn't want Trent looking at them in their underwear. The other part is thinking she doesn't want to look at them running around in their panties, either.

"Duct tape," Ken says as they start upstairs. "Works wonders."

"So... they're wearing duct tape skirts?" Emily asks, trying not to snicker and failing.

"Yep, duct taped skirts. Nico's idea."

Emily decides she likes Nico, a lot.

★ ★ ★

My dad just totally caught me flirting. I'm pretty sure that my neck is red with embarrassment, but he hasn't said anything and I think that Emily never realized I was flirting in the first place, so... I might have gotten away with it--

Liz catches up as we reach the top floor of the experiment room and drapes an arm over my shoulders. "She's cute, huh?" she whispers evilly. "That little trick with the doppelganger and the skirts, I like her!"

Nope, totally busted. "Liz," I say.

"So you two are dating for real, right?" she whispers. "She'll make a cute little Liberty girl. Hey, that means I have two nieces!"

"No it doesn't!" I hiss. "Not yet, anyway," I add silently, glancing at Emily.

"You dog, you," Liz says with a wide grin, elbowing me in the gut.

"Nah, it might just be me," I say silently, knowing I look flustered. Liz is good at getting to you. I think she practices in her free time.

"Now, if I could get your attention," Nico says, making all of us turn. "This is where we'll work on mad science, so you'll see several precautions in place. There's a steady supply of fire retardant hoses--no, not canisters, I think the hoses will prove useful quickly, considering. We have eyebath stations for the random acid incident, a fully equipped first aid kit at each station, and a nurse's office upstairs and downstairs. All the basic science materials can be found in the heavily secure locker room seen to your left, and more can be attained as is needed."

"Is it just me or does Nico seem way more enthusiastic about this building than he should be?" Dad asks dryly. Nico grins at him.

"You might have noticed that next to the deconstruction area there is a large, two level high empty area below that has only rocks and dirt in it," Nico goes on. "That is where I'll be training my kid, Sunny. Up here is where I'll be training Zoe. And anyone else that shows mad science and technological inclinations."

"Wait--you seriously built an entire building just for us?" Zoe asks.

"It's my land, my school, what's going to stop me?" Nico asks bluntly. "But more than just you will require areas like this, so it'll be fine. Added bonus? If they complain about favoritism I might get fired!"

"I think it'll take more than that to get you fired," Frank says. "Frankly, I don't want to buy all of this unless I have to."

"Good point," Nico says. "Well, with that, shall we move to the third building?"

"And what's in the third building?" Frank asks.

"The cafeteria's on the bottom floor along with a lounge area, the second and third floors are dormitories," Nico says. "So if any of the students need a place to live, they can have one. The fourth floor is storage."

I can almost hear Emily's shock at that statement. I feel a bit shocked, myself, honestly. So... Emily is going to move out? In some ways I guess that's a good thing for me--I mean, you really get strange looks if you're trying to date the house guest, right? But on the other hand, just how long would she stick around if she was all on her own?

"Of course, we'll need a dorm manager, which might be a bit tough to get," Nico says. "Right now all we have is Emily--and the two brunettes if they decide to come."

"Yeah, like we'd come here," I hear the shorter one mutter under her breath.

"Looks like the dorms will be empty for a while--"

"Wait!" Emily says. "Maybe I should move in. You know, because this is the entire reason I was brought here and I--I'd rather not cause more problems for the Styles family--"

"We'll discuss it later," Dad says.

"Well, then, let's take a look at the cafeteria and dorms, then head to the field," Nico says, heading for the stairs. I follow along with my hands in my pockets, wondering if I should at least ask her out for ice cream or something before she runs away to hide in the dorms.

Then I remember I'm grounded for flicking the brunette. There goes that idea.

"We are NOT letting my sweet little girl live all alone in the dorms!" Mom says as soon as we get back to the apartments, not even bothering to lower her voice. Everyone in the apartment building should have heard that, considering who all lives there. Including Emily, since she's right behind Mom.

"But it's the perfect solution," Emily says. "I mean, I came here to go to school, not to rely on a family I've only just met and--and I did that thing today--"

"Oh, honey, I would have done it myself at your age," Mom says, waving it off. "Those two little brats need a good talking to, if you ask me!"

"Jeanie," Dad says mildly, "I think it's time for a family conference."

"I'll be in my room--" Emily says, only to be jerked to a halt as Dad grabs her hand.

"No you don't," he says. "You're going to sit on the couch and listen to us very carefully." He tugs her along behind him, stopping in front of the couch, where she promptly plops down in the middle seat and crosses her arms over her chest. I drop down in front of the couch next to her legs, just waiting for it. "Now, I understand that you were looking for revenge for what happened in the past," Dad says, standing in front of her. "Did it feel good?"

"It--for a bit?" Emily admits. "They deserved it," she adds darkly.

"But do you really think what you did today profits you?" Dad asks.

"What, like it makes me money?" she asks.

"No, like it makes you a better person," he says.

Emily flushes and looks down, muttering a quiet "No."

"Emily, we know that your past wasn't good," he goes on. "Losing your parents so young, it breaks my heart. And the situation after that--I know we can't change those things. But what we can do, and what we want to do, is to make your *now* better, to make your future something worth looking forward to." He gets on his knees in front of her, looking her straight in the eyes. "Emily, honey, we forgive you for what you did today. We like you very much already, and honestly, we don't want you running off because you think you don't belong, or you're not good enough, or anything you might be thinking right now."

Mom drops down on the couch on the other side and pulls Emily into a hug. "We want you here," she says, rubbing Emily's back. "We want you safe and surrounded by love and not in a position where you feel threatened or scared. Even when you're a working cape, sweetie, we're going to make sure you're equipped to deal with it."

"I--" I start out before stopping myself.

"Trent?" Mom asks.

"I think she'd make a good partner," I say, looking at Emily. "I mean, I'm a tank--two tanks is overkill, which is why you two stick to traffic and major events, right? But if I'm going to be paired up against Max--wouldn't it be good to have a spy type for my partner?"

Emily turns bright red. Like so red that her ears are red. Huh, I think, feeling a bit embarrassed just because she is, maybe she did notice the flirting.

"Emily, do you think that would work for you?" Dad asks.

"I dunno," she mutters, glancing at me. "I guess?"

"How about we ask for you two to be trained as a team just to try it out?" Mom says, looking excited. "I'm sure Nico and Liz and I can come up with something that will work!"

I watch Emily. There are several different emotions crossing her face all at once, so I've got no idea what she really thinks of this idea. Maybe she's only going along with it because she feels guilty... I'll have to ask her later, when the parents aren't plotting the rest of her life with me.

The tailor comes and goes, taking my measurements and consulting with me and Mom for a few minutes. Night comes. I haven't even managed to get my tank-top on (boxers, yes, thank God,) when Ditto pops in, already sitting on my bed. I look at her. "Seriously, Ditto, your timing is terrible," I complain as I tug my tank-top over my head. "I'd almost swear you do it on purpose, too," I add.

"I have no idea what you mean," Ditto says innocently. That means she's up to something. "So what's all this about being partners, anyway? We are our own partner!"

"Well yeah," I admit, dropping down on the head of the bed, a good three feet away from where she's sitting. "But I'm willing to work with both of you! Two partners for the price of one, right? I can have you scout one part of the building while Emily checks another part--it's like having an entire team in one little package!"

"And what about you, huh? Your big job is to just barge in and destroy things, right?" she asks dryly.

"Exactly!" I say with a huge grin. "Best job ever. It's what I'm built for, too."

"You're just trying to look good," she mutters darkly.

"Nah," I say. "You know... as long as I'm going up against Max and not a serious super villain, which is probably what I'll be doing most of my life when there are no major problems to clean up, well, it's more like a football game than a war, right? He'll probably talk Zoe into being his partner, so I'll have tons of massive robots to beat up, too. Sounds fun, huh?" I'm looking forward to it, at least.

"I could pop into the robots and break something inside," Ditto says, her dark blue eyes gleaming. "But I like Zoe!" she says abruptly, looking guilty. "I don't want to hurt her--"

"Eh, breaking her toys won't hurt her," I say, waving it off. "You've already decided you like her?"

"She blew up Allie's phone for me," Ditto says happily. "She's pretty easy to read. With Allie and Kelly they always tried to pretend that they weren't mad, but it's really hard to pretend that when things are blowing up, right?"

Her logic is a bit flawed, but it sounds good enough, I guess. Zoe is only confusing when it comes to Max, as far as I can tell. "What about Max and Sunny?" I ask.

"Mmmm... I don't know," she admits. "I've not really talked to Sunny, but you like him, right? And Max is kind of scary, if you think about it. Are you sure Zoe should be going out with him? He's a super villain--"

I hear someone laughing upstairs and wonder if we're being spied on by the entire apartment. Maybe I'm just paranoid, but I doubt it. "So's her dad," I point out.

"But he's an ex super villain, right? That means he's no longer bad--and he made the sisters duct tape their skirts, which is great! They looked so stupid!"

"That doesn't make him a good guy, Ditto," I drawl. "That just means he didn't feel like taking his shirt off for them."

"I think it does!" she says stubbornly.

I'm about to argue with her when Emily steps into the room wearing a pair of flag striped PJ bottoms and a blue camisole that has Star Spangled written in cursive across the front and surrounded by white stars. "When'd you get those?" I ask her curiously.

"Liz gave them to me," she says as she takes her spot at the bottom of my bed, hugging her knees to her chest. I doubt she'd be running around in them if she didn't like them, and Ditto just fuzzed out for a second, and is now wearing the exact same thing. Yep, she likes them. "So Allie and Kelly aren't coming back," she says.

"That we know of," I agree.

"But... we'll probably run into them when we start working as capes, right?"

"Maybe," I admit.

"Do you really think I'll make a good partner?" she asks, looking up at me hesitantly. Oh man is she cute. It's like a one-two hit when Ditto looks at me in a similar manner. Surround sound cuteness, or something--which I will NEVER say out loud, so keep it to yourself, okay? I'm barely restraining from tripping over myself trying to assure her that she'd make an awesome(ly cute) partner right now. I'm already picturing her in a white and blue uniform, hopefully with a skirt, when I stop myself.

This is serious time.

I look at her for a moment. "Do you think you'd be a good partner?" I ask, trying to think like Dad. It's not as easy as it sounds, although I've been following his line of thought all my life, practically. He's the one that taught me most of everything I know and believe, after all. I figure you can't get a better guy to follow than one that practices what he preaches (literally) right? Not that I'd ever tell him that.

"I... would want to be," she says quietly. "But what if they're right? What if I am too wild, or too much of a liar or too weak? What happens if I get caught?"

"Of all the kids in the group," I say, "you're the least likely to get caught. You're built for it, remember?"

"Well, yeah..."

"And if you get caught in our usual thing, well... I figure Max will tie you up in the corner and use you as leverage against me for some dramatic set-up," I say plainly. "He's the type that will offer you cupcakes or a smoothie while you wait for me to come save you," I add dryly. I've gotten to know Max pretty well, after all. I can honestly say that he would do exactly that, or something equally ridiculous. "Then you just need to summon Ditto to cut your ropes like you did the skirts today."

"You're right!" she says, practically bouncing as she realizes it. "That'd be fun! Oh, but I'd probably wait for the cupcakes first," she adds thoughtfully.

This time I'm positive I hear my Dad laugh. But then again, the door is open and we're not bothering to whisper, so I'm not surprised. I can't help the grin that crosses my face, either, because I can clearly picture her demanding cupcakes in exchange for staying long enough for Max to film her acting as hostage.

"But there is one thing I've been wondering," she says.

"What's that?"

"Well... I just wonder if I can't make Ditto look like someone else," she says hesitantly. "I mean, I've tried and it doesn't work all that great, but they're going to teach us, right? It'd be really cool if I could make doppelgangers of other people!"

"That would be amazing," I say. "Man I can't wait for school to start!" I never thought I'd say that in my life.

Kelly and Allie stare up at the old, abandoned looking apartment building for a long moment. "This is where they came, right?" Kelly says.

"Yeah, this is it."

"Do we know what floor she's on?"

"Not a clue," Allie admits. "But if we could find her window, we could sneak in and deal with her properly. That was my favorite skirt!" She starts forward, only to be hauled to a stop by her sister.

"Don't," Kelly says. She crouches down, picking up a stone and tossing it at the building. Light flashes where it hits the wall of lasers, and the rock is blown up into tiny dust particles. "That crazy super villain's been here," she says darkly. "Maybe if we dig under..."

"Whatcha doing?"

The two jerk, turning around quickly to look at the large man in the white uniform that is standing behind them. "Te--Technico?" Allie yelps.

"Hmm?" the man asks, stepping forward so the moonlight hits him. His hair is white with a streak of black. "You're looking for Technico?" he asks.

"No!" Kelly says, backing up. The world seems to twist around them and she feels sick to her stomach as the colors of everything around her try to invert. "We're just--just passing by!"

"Oh," he says. "Do you live here?"

"No! She just said we're passing through," Allie says. "We're not from around here, so we need to be getting home--" She turns, grabbing her sister's arm and tugging, only to stop as a woman lands in front of them, her hair not even mussed by her flying.

"Hello, little supers," she says. "We couldn't help but notice that you seem to be lost. Why don't we help you find your way?"

"Y--you--" Allie whispers. "What are you two?"

The glowing eyes turn up at the corners as Star Born smiles.

Morning comes. It's Sunday, so Dad and Mom go to visit the church at the new meeting spot (someone's house) while I'm stuck here at the apartment building with the rest of the group. I feel a bit strange not going to church, I decide as I lay in my bed. I guess I can't complain, though, since we don't know if that one lady is still around looking for me. And since I've got a battle with Max this afternoon, I should probably rest up for it.

"Are you going to stay in bed all day?" Emily asks, opening my door and walking in as if she owns the room. "Zoe invited us upstairs for breakfast. They're making pancakes!"

"Sounds good," I say, "but let me get a shower first."

"Then I'm going up before you do," she says before rushing off. I climb out of bed and head for the bathroom to get cleaned up. I finish my shower, get dressed, and head upstairs. The Masters' apartment is busy as usual, with people either cooking or hanging out on the couches. Emily's in the kitchen with Zoe, wearing an apron and everything as she helps get the table ready. Sunny's passed out on the couch and Nico is sitting next to him, staring at a laptop with a scowl on his face.

"Hey," I say as I enter, heading for the kitchen. "Need any help?" I ask.

"Can you get the orange juice out?" Zoe asks as she flips pancakes.

"Zoe, did you go outside the apartment last night?" Nico calls over.

"No, I didn't," she calls back. "Why?"

"Because there's about a ten minute section in the security tape that isn't showing," he says, tapping on the keyboard. "It's like interference... huh."

"Can you get through it?" Zoe asks, looking extremely curious.

"Maybe, give me a bit of time to unscramble it," he says. He stops, though, as the laptop beeps. "Frank and Max are coming," he tells us. "You might make some extra pancakes, kiddo."

"Yeah," Zoe says, going back to cooking. The door opens a few minutes later and Max steps in, stepping out of the way for Frank.

"We've got a bit of a problem," Frank says.

"What's that?" Nico asks, still tapping on his laptop.

"We escorted the two girls home last night, but their parents say they never came home," Frank says. "I've sent out a search party--" He stops as his phone rings, pulling it out of his pocket and answering. "Yes? Yes... so you did find them... I'll come now," he says. "We've found them."

"Where were they?" Emily asks.

"Two blocks from here," Frank says.

"Take me with you," Emily says, taking her apron off and putting it over the nearest chair. Frank looks at her, and then looks at me.

"Trent, you come, too," he says, heading out. Emily chases after him and I follow behind, not too surprised when the rest of the group follows me. Even Sunny's woken up enough to come with us--much to my shock.

"I'm not sure I like letting you all out in public right now," Nico says darkly as we head out of the apartment one by one, each stepping on the lighted footprints. We follow Frank as he heads two blocks away to a large circle of black hummers, making his way to the center of the circle.

The two sisters lay piled up on the street corner, unmoving. I have to move closer to hear their heartbeats. The heartbeats are off slightly, and I grab Emily before she says anything. Frank crouches down next to them, touching one forehead. "I see," he says a second later. "Take them to the Hall, have them checked over," he says to one of the black suits that are waiting for their orders.

"What happened to them?" Emily asks.

"Something like what happened to the principal, I'm afraid," Frank says quietly. "Now, back to the apartment building. We have a fight to get ready for."

"Dad, are you certain we should do this now?" Max asks.

"We are opening the school tomorrow, Max. Regardless of these two idiots running back here without my permission, the school will still start. I was informed by several witnesses that they were delivered safely and promptly home. That they are here now means that they came by their own choice. And I, personally, told them that it wasn't safe to be here on their own."

"But--" Emily starts out. "What about their parents?"

"They will be informed," Frank says. "Emily, what--or should I say who do you think they came back for?" he asks her.

Emily looks at the girls. "Yeah, I know," she says. "But their parents never did anything bad to me--"

"They let it happen," Frank says coldly. "Any super worth their title would notice abuse in their own house." And I suddenly realize just how high up on Frank's "Do not approve" list the family is. Emily might have wanted revenge, but Frank doing *nothing* is a far worse revenge than Emily would ever think of. I know this for a fact.

We watch silently as the sisters are taken away and I pull Emily into a hug. "I didn't do this," she says abruptly. "Everyone knows that, right? I'm the one that cut their skirts, but I didn't do this."

"We know that," Frank says. "I read their minds, remember?"

"Okay," she says, looking back as the black ambulance drives off with the sisters inside. "They wouldn't have gotten anywhere," she says abruptly. "They would have been stopped at the security system, right?"

"Yes. But they know about the school," Frank says. "We should assume that whoever did this knows, as well."

"It should be interesting," Nico says.

Emily moves a little closer, not saying anything or even looking at me, but I can feel a fine tremor running through her. "I know," I say quietly, "this is more than you wanted."

She nods, and then shakes her head, a tear escaping. "I did want this sometimes, I wanted them beat up, or something. That's why I feel so guilty, I think."

CHAPTER SIX

The suit that the tailor came up with is more like an army uniform than the traditional tights. I've got a pair of clunky work boots that are surprisingly light, and pants in the same dark blue as the sleeveless top, although they have a red and white stripe pattern down one leg that looks like a flag flapping. The traditional spot on the chest is covered with a highly stylized image that resembles an eagle in white and red. A clunky belt goes around my waist and although I'm not wearing sleeves, I have tough worker type dark blue gloves.

Emily is staring at me as I tug the gloves on. "What?" I ask, feeling a bit embarrassed.

"I was expecting a cape," she says.

"No capes," I say. "Never saw the point of a cape."

"Because you're a super?" she offers, picking up the dark blue fitted mask and handing it to me. I slip it on, making sure it attaches with the makeup glue, then stand, blinking as she pulls out what looks to be my mother's cell phone and takes several pictures. "Jeanie said I had to take them," she says.

"She's going to be watching, though," I say.

"Well, yeah, but she's already at the fight sight eating McDonalds," Emily explains. "Since that's the easiest way to be there without getting noticed."

"Yeah, yeah," I say.

"You're supposed to pose," she prompts.

"I'm not going to pose!" I say, trying not to laugh.

"You've got to pose! Do some heroic pose like sticking one hand up in the air or something," she says.

"How is sticking one arm up in the air heroic?" I ask, giving in to the laughter. She snaps another picture and grins at me. "If you go along with the training as a team, you'll be in a uniform that goes along with this one," I tell her. "Be grateful we don't get stuck with capes."

"I want stars on mine," she decides.

"You wanna be a mini-Mom, or something?" I tease.

"No, but I like stars! Or maybe stripes," she says thoughtfully.

"We'll figure it out when you're actually going to start," I say, heading out of the apartment with her behind me. "We'll have to get your stripes fixed."

"I like my stripes!" she protests.

"I mean darker, maybe add some white, too," I say. "I like the stripes too." She blushes and I can't help but grin as we head down the stairs. Nico's waiting at the front door, where he hands me a new transmitter.

"Emily, you can run, right?"

"Yeah?" she says.

"Then here," he says, dropping a hand on her head. "Keep your head low and keep up. I hear you'll be training as Trent's sidekick," he adds as we start out through the security system.

"Partner," she says. "I'm going to be his partner."

"Ahhh, that serious, huh?" Nico teases me as I step off of the last glowing footstep.

"Shuddup," I mutter, knowing I look even redder in all this blue. "Don't we have work to do?"

"Yep." We take off, but I can't help but glance back at Emily every few minutes to make sure she's doing okay. She's only fourteen, after all. She looks a bit tired as we reach the fight sight and I motion for her to go over to the McDonalds where Mom and Dad are sitting at one of the outdoor tables. Max is already there. He's got a mic. God help us all, Max with a mic.

"You people are the privileged few that will see my new headquarters being built!" he says over the mic. "Of course that means I'm going to have to kill you all afterwards--it's nothing personal, of course, but I can't have any witnesses."

I'm not going to laugh. I'm *not* going to laugh. He likes his job WAY too much.

"Hey!" I bellow.

"Oh? What's this? Hey, did you come to help with the building?" Max asks over the mic. "Because you look like a construction worker. Mind you, I don't pay more than minimum wage--"

I grab a large slat of concrete from the pile, then spin, throwing it like a discus straight at him. Max yelps and drops the mic, dodging at the last second. I can't help it--I grab the fallen mic. What? It's too good an opportunity to pass up!

"You're done, Maximum," I say over the mic. "You keep saying you're the new face of supers, but you know what? I don't like your face enough to let it represent us."

"Wait--hey, you stole my mic!" Max says. "Gimme back my mic!"

"No way, I like the mic," I say. "I'm here to stop you, Maximum, whether you like it or--" I see his hand move and I'm expecting the bus to hit me from behind--sort of. Thankfully Nico warns me with a quick "behind you." I grunt, losing my hold on the mic as the bus sends me a few steps forward. I can hear the metal screeching when I dig my feet into the ground. When my body stops giving the metal has to start.

Max's got the mic again. "Geez, man, you wrecked my bus!" he says over the mic. Just for that I turn, punching the bus and sending it flying several feet before it falls. "I was fond of that bus!" he protests. So I have to run over, pick the bus up and toss it straight at him. This time it hits him full on and I race forward, grabbing the mic as it falls to the ground again.

Nico's laughing. I can't help but grin as I bring the mic up. "If you like it so much I'm happy I can give it back," I say. The cops have shown up by now and are surrounding the area, keeping the norms from getting too close. "Ladies and gentlemen, on behalf of all supers, especially the next generation, I'd like to apologize for Maximum--"

The bus is shoved up and Max climbs out from under it, dusting himself off. Then, a bit to my surprise, he launches himself straight at me, slamming into me with the weight of a meteor. Him and his gravity powers, I think as the breath is knocked out of me. The mic goes flying and we launch into a flat out, knock down, brawl. He's cheating, of course, he's using his gravity powers to make his hits heavier and mine lighter, but it looks good--that's what matters.

We've got choppers flying overhead, and news stations recording us, and I can't help but think that if they wanted a poster boy matchup, they got one. By the time this video gets out on Hero TV we'll be having would-be supers of both sides asking their parents if they can come--

Max goes flying backwards with my next hit, an uppercut to the jaw, and I hear Nico over the transmitter. "Nice fall. Make sure you land properly--good. Now grab the mic, and make your final threats before flying off."

The mic goes flying into Max's hand as he staggers dramatically to his feet. "You might have won this one, kid," he says--oh crap, I forgot to introduce myself, "but this isn't over. I'm going to get even, got it? This isn't over!" Then he flies off so fast that the wind messes up my hair.

"He took the mic," I mutter.

"What do you expect from Max? He's a ham," Nico drawls. "Now go check on the norms, be sure to pat little kids on the head while you're at it."

"I forgot to give my name, though."

"It'll be fine," he says as I head for the crowd pressing against the cops.

"Is everyone okay?" I ask.

"They're fine. You did good, kid," the cop nearest me says. "What's your name?"

"Liberty," I say with a grin. "Kid Liberty." I crouch down as I see a little boy reaching an arm past the cop's leg. "Hey," I say, taking the tiny hand. The little black boy looks up at me with huge eyes, and then grins at me, showing he's missing a tooth. I hear photos being snapped. "You didn't get scared, did you?" I ask him.

"No," he whispers.

"Good. You're going to be a good boy, right?" I ask.

"Yes," he says.

"Good." I stand, salute the cops, and race away.

"That was AWESOME!" Max says over the transmitter. "Definitely a good introduction."

"You're both hams," Nico says with amusement, "but not bad.

You definitely made an impact. Now make sure you don't get followed--Max, hop a state or two before coming back, Trent, do a few rounds and change before going back to the apartments. We'll be keeping an eye on you both."

"Where's Emily?" I ask.

"With your parents."

"Where's Zoe?" Max asks.

"With me. She says you did good."

"Good," Max says. "Think my fall was dramatic enough?"

"I think you just didn't want hit in the face again," I drawl.

"How do you think I keep my extremely cute girlfriend, man? I'm attached to this face!" I'm heading south, passing a few small towns absently, planning on turning around soon, but something catches my eye. I slow, and then stop, watching as a pair of capes fly overhead. "Hey, Max? Did your dad say anything about visiting capes?"

"Today? No, not that I know of."

"We've got two headed straight for Kansas City right now. One male, one female--both in traditional good guy garb," I say, watching them for a moment. "I think..."

"It must be the parents," Nico says. "Come back, boys, meet at the Hall--Max you might want to change clothes first."

"Yes sir," I say, starting back for Kansas City.

The Hall is a place I visited a few times as I was little--well, more than a few times. I've been babysat by more than half of the major players in the Central Hall. Falconess still gives me a hard time about changing my diapers whenever she comes over for a barbecue, and Mega has played catch with me a million times over. Honestly, I'm surprised I'd never met Max before he transferred into my school for a day or two. Then again, Max's entire existence was a bit of a mystery to the Hall until he decided to make his debut as a super villain.

I head through the underground entrance, nodding to the

guard and checking in as usual--face scan, fingerprint scan, all the stuff you have to do to get into the not-for-public part of the building. I finally step into the main room, where the two capes from earlier are screaming at Frank.

"What have you done to our daughters?" the father bellows. He's taller than Frank, broader than Frank, and usually a situation like this would be one sided, but Frank's just standing there, waiting for them to finish. I see Nico sitting at the large C shaped table that surrounds the floor they're standing on. He's got his feet propped up on the table, which is probably outraging every assistant in the area, and is typing away on his laptop.

He stops and I hear noise coming from the speakers, too quiet for the screaming parents to hear. It's the sisters talking, I realize. He's unscrambled the feed from the apartment's security camera. "Frank," he says.

"Excuse me for a moment," Frank says. The father grabs the front of his uniform, hauling him off his feet.

"I think not," the man says. "Do you know who we are?"

"You are Allie and Kelly's parents, Geoff and Marlina Behts, AKA Crank and Juxta, B class supers from the South Branch," Frank says. "Do you know who I am?"

I can see sweat appear on Crank's face and how he has to force his fingers to let go of the uniform, which Frank straightens quickly before heading to Nico. "Found him," Nico says.

"I see," Frank says. "I'm afraid there's no doubt now, is there?"

"Look like it," Nico says. "I can't say that I've ever wanted a brother," he adds darkly.

"And the distortion?" Frank asks, ignoring how the mother is trying to see what they're doing.

"Have you found out what happened to my girls?" she demands. "It has something to do with Emily, doesn't it? She's so small but she's vicious--"

"You will refrain from speaking this instant," Frank says in a tone that I'm sure is a mental command as well. Her mouth snaps shut, but her eyes look shocked. "Trent," he says, "Max."

I glance behind me, seeing Max head for us in civvies. "Nico's unscrambled the feed," I tell him.

"Who did it?" Max asks.

"It looks like the same man Zoe described from earlier... and a woman. Trent, can you come here?" Nico asks. I head over, looking over his shoulder at the woman on the screen. "Is this the woman from your old school?"

The glowing eyes, the perfect hair, the pencil thin skirt. "Yes," I say, "that's her."

"Frank, do you recognize her?" Nico asks.

"No, but I'll have my people look into it," Frank says. "We've finally got a lead. Now, to deal with you two," he goes on, turning to the two parents. "Your children are in the healing ward. They're recovering well, and as far as we can tell have only suffered concussions and shock from their experiences."

"Oh thank God," the father breathes out.

"Except," Frank interrupts, "somehow they no longer have their abilities. We're trying to find out what's happened to them, but for the moment your daughters are norms."

"Wh--what?"

"It could be any number of things, and honestly they're cluttering up my healing ward, so I suggest you take them home to your own Hall and deal with it there," Frank says, totally unsympathetically. "If our tests come up with any results we will pass it on to your Hall. If not, well I suggest they think a lot harder before they gang up on a young cape, regardless of how developed her powers are at the time."

"Our daughters were only defending themselves!" the father snarls.

"From a fourteen year old girl who was barely starting to show signs," Frank says coldly. "Two on one is not defending, two on one is a crime."

"You don't know Emily!" the mother says. "She's a wild animal! She's rabid!"

"Get out," I snarl, startling myself as much as I do everyone else in the room. "Get out of my Hall! Nobody talks about Emily like that! You just stood there and let them gang up on her--you've got no right to don a mask!"

"Who do you think you are, telling us what to do?" the father demands, turning on me. "You have nothing to do with this situation!"

"Yes he does," I hear my father say from behind me, "because Emily is his future partner." I turn, seeing Dad and Mom both in full uniform, with Emily standing in front of them. Emily looks like she's been slapped.

"Emily," I say, holding out a hand to her, "come here." She hesitates for a mere second before stepping forward and taking my hand. "This isn't a wild animal," I say clearly. "This is a girl who's lost everything, and when she turned to you, you betrayed her. You accuse her of having something to do with this. You accuse her of assaulting your *two* older and physically stronger daughters. You're as bad as they are. And even with all that, she still cried when she saw your daughters the way they wound up."

"You have no idea what happened--" the mother starts out.

"Do you want me to find out?" Frank says. "Because I can. And if I know for certain that you were aware of what was going on and did nothing to stop it, I will have you thrown into the cape cells for being an accomplice to child cape abuse."

"You--she--" the father splutters.

"I believe Kid Liberty has already told you to leave," Frank says. "I suggest you gather your children and do exactly that."

"Wait," Emily say. The room seems to go still as she takes a step forward. "Mastermental... I don't think it's right, not trying your hardest to find out what they did to take their powers," she says quietly. "Regardless of--of the past, it's just... we need to find out how to fix it, right? In case it happens to someone else."

"She acts like this in front of you, but--" the father says. I take a step forward, my hands fisting at my sides, only to stop as I realize Emily's hanging onto my waist, trying to stop me.

"Don't," she says, looking up at me. "Does this make you a better person?"

"It might make him one," I say coldly.

"Trent," Dad says quietly before stepping forward. "We are truly sorry for what's happened to your daughters," he tells the two in front of us. "But Emily has nothing to do with what happened-- except in one way. Your daughters came here for her, and spoke about it as they went on the tour. We all heard it. And since we've clearly established that they came back after being delivered by a small group of assistants, they came back for her, as well. That, in no way, shape or form, is Emily's fault."

"America's Son," Crank snarls. "I thought you were always out for justice, regardless of who the wrongdoer is--"

"I am. If this were Emily's fault I would make sure she was dealt with. But trying to blame a fourteen year old child for your daughters' mistakes is not acceptable to me."

"Geoff, don't," Marlina says, grabbing her husband's arm. "You can't take on an entire Liberty family."

"Liberty--" he stops, his eyes falling on me. "I should have realized," he says. "We're leaving. But this isn't the end of it, Mastermental. I fully hold you responsible for what's happened. If my daughters never regain their powers, it's your fault."

"No," Nico says, "it would be the Superior line's fault."

"Superior?" Crank asks, going pale. "Who are you?"

"Technico, first son--I assume, at least--of Superior himself. And had you been calmer you would have seen exactly what happened to your children. To be honest it's not completely Superior fault," he says thoughtfully. "But I have no idea who she is, and since she's working with him, well, he's as good a choice to blame as any. If you really desire revenge, go after this man." He turns the laptop around, showing a screenshot of a man that looks exactly like him, but like a photo negative, with the colors backwards. "But you won't win."

"He's a villain, isn't he? Good always wins--" the father starts out.

"He is a *Superior brat*," Nico says coldly. "Good or bad or what you think counts as 'good,' even, doesn't matter when you're that outranked. If you want to see how you stand up to a son of Superior, I'll be happy to show you." He's put the laptop down and is on his feet, still wearing his civvies. There's no built in defense in that t-shirt he's wearing, but I don't think he needs it for this one.

"Nico," Frank says. "Sit back down."

Nico looks at him, and I can see him debating on whether to obey or not. Instead of doing either, he turns for the exit. "I'll lead them to the healing ward. I need to check on Jack, anyway."

"How is Jack doing?" I ask.

"We've gotten it to where he can breathe on his own," Nico says, "but he's still unconscious and unresponsive. It's going to take more work." He looks at the parents, looking impatient. "Follow me."

They hesitate before nodding reluctantly and Nico leads them out of the room, leaving the laptop on the table. For a moment the room is silent, and then I feel Emily's head bump against my chest and look down. She's shivering. I wrap my arms around her, tugging her close. Her arms go around my waist and I know she's trying her hardest not to cry. How can they think that this girl is rabid? What just happened almost broke her. For how long has she been this close to the edge?

"You did good," I say, feeling a tiny bit awkward at this happening when surrounded by people. "You did real good," I repeat, rubbing her back.

"They--they--" she whimpers. "They thought--that I--"

"I know," I say. "They're wrong. We all know it. Do you want me to make them regret it?" I ask. "Because I can."

She shakes her head against my chest before hugging tighter, as if trying to force me to stay right where I am. I look up, not surprised as Mom and Dad step in front of me, turning this into a group hug. I glance over at Frank and Max, who are standing to the side, having a silent conversation, no doubt. They have the same expressions on their faces and suddenly I see the family resemblance. It's a bit terrifying, if you think about it, the idea of these two teamed up together. But then Frank changes the subject.

"I believe this is as good a time as any," he says, making us step back and turn to him. Somehow Emily has transferred from me to my mother and is cuddled up against her side like a chick under a wing. "Since we have established the two boys as enemies, I would appreciate you keeping up the rivalry in the school. And I know that you and Zoe are friends, Emily, but a bit of feuding, or perhaps trying to talk her out of dating a super villain might be expected. It will, of course, be for show, but--"

"I--I don't mind if Zoe knows it's just play acting, right?" Emily says, frowning.

"She will be informed," Frank says with a smile.

"I'm looking forward to it," Max says, grinning at me. "Team captains, right?" he says.

"I get Sunny," I say quickly.

"I'm keeping Zoe. But we need another super villain or undecided if that's the case," Max says. "Since you're obviously keeping Emily, too."

"Ah, yes. The one I'm planning on recruiting hasn't called back yet, but I've heard from Panther. Of course it was delivered as a threat letter shortly after the fight, you can't expect a traditionalist like Panther to do anything else, but he's asked for his son and daughter to be admitted into the school. He wants both to be properly trained super villains. Sadly, I could only accept the daughter for the moment."

"And why is that?" Max asks.

"Because the son is only three years old. The daughter is fourteen, almost fifteen. According to tradition, she should be called Adanna, now that there's a son to inherit the family name, but for most of her life she was called Cub. His threat letter is extremely informative. His wife sent a text, though, saying that she would rather her daughter choose her own path. As far as we're concerned you can both try and sway her to your sides."

"Do you have a picture?" Sunny asks.

"Of course. I've been watching Cub quite closely for a while. She's a shape shifter," Frank says, pulling out a piece of paper from his pocket and handing it over to Max. Max looks at it curiously for a long moment before handing it over to me. The black girl in the picture is thin and wiry looking, but her face is striking, even though it looks like she's trying to dress and look like a boy. She has high cheekbones and tilted eyes and a wide, full mouth that's set in a threatening scowl.

"What does she shift into?" Emily asks, peeking at the picture I'm holding.

"What else? A panther, of course. Enhanced speed, hearing, agility, all the things that made her the perfect heir for the Panther name except for her gender," Frank says. "She's trained since before she could walk in bō staff fighting and hand to hand combat. I was hoping your showing would get her, especially since she lives so close."

"It sounds like she's already well trained," Max says.

"Unfortunately she's having quite a bit of trouble with her shape shifting," Frank says. "And with the new brother, well, she's at a disadvantage. I expect you to treat her well," he adds, looking pointedly at Max, "since officially she'll be on your team, so to say."

"I've always admired Panther," Max says, "she'll be fine."

"She'll be there tomorrow for the first day," Frank says. "Now, if I could speak with Emily for a moment?" he adds. "Privately?"

I look at Emily, who looks a bit worried. I nod, heading for the exit with the others. I can't help but feel like I should stay, though, as the door closes behind the last of the assistants. I can't hear a thing from inside the room.

★ ★ ★

"Now, seeing as you're no longer in hearing distance of the Liberty family," Frank says as he turns to the little redhead. "Tell me what you would have done with that family."

"Wh--what? I don't think it's really right about the little brother, but it frees her up to--"

"Not that family," Frank says, "the Beht family."

"Oh. Them." Emily looks down, staring at her feet for a long moment before speaking. "I don't like them," she says quietly. "I don't like how he just assumed he was good because he's called a hero, or how they just assumed their daughters were right--I don't like them at all. I'm glad I don't have to pretend to live with them anymore," she says fiercely.

"Do you want them out of the super business?" he asks.

"What?" Emily asks, shocked. "I can't really decide that--"

"But I can," he says. "Although this might come to a surprise to many, I am still the official head of the Hall--regardless of what branch it might be. I can fire them. Their hall leader might protest, and I might have some red tape to cut through, but within a month or less they will lose their backing as Hall members. I cannot stop them from going vigilante, of course, but it is not a very nice world for vigilante heroes."

Emily looks at the door, and then looks back at him. "I... I don't like what they did in their personal life, but I never heard about them doing bad things in their cape life," she says finally. "There aren't really that many heroes, right? I mean, when you think about how many norms there are--can you--I don't know, stick them on some sort of fire fighting duty or traffic accident duty instead? Oh, or something really, really nasty, like sewer patrol or something! Something that needs to be done, but really sucks to do! Where they never show up in newspapers or anything cool like Trent just did!"

Frank looks at her for a moment, and then starts to laugh at the sight of her wicked grin. He reaches up, messing up her short red hair with a fond smile. "Consider it done," he says. "You know, I think that you will be an excellent addition to the Liberty family."

"You mean because I'm going to be Trent's partner?" she asks. "But that's not really enough to let me use the super hero family name, right? I mean, I'm part of the Divine family, not that anyone knows us hardly... or me, I should say."

"In time," Frank says. "Maybe you should consider using it in your name? As a tribute."

"If I can live up to it," she says.

"Something like Divine Justice," Frank adds. "Or Justice Divine."

Emily smiles a little. "Yeah, maybe. So I can go now, right? I've got school in the morning."

"Of course. Thank you for your very helpful input, Emily," he says. "I'll get that set up now."

"Okay!" she says, grinning from ear to ear as she heads out the door. She stops, though, with her hand on the handle. "But... please find out how to fix the girls, okay?"

"Oh?"

"Yeah. I want them doing sewer duty, too." He's still laughing as she slips out the door and heads straight for the family waiting for her with anxious expressions. Ken's the first to react.

"And?" he asks.

"Sewer duty for Geoff and Marlina!" she says, looking quite important. "He offered to have them canned, but we need heroes, right? So I thought they should do something that needs to be done--but is really nasty, instead." She grins as Jeanie tugs her into a hug, kissing her on the forehead.

"A very fitting decision," Ken says. "There are a lot of really nasty jobs out there that need to be done, and maybe it will teach them a bit of humility. But sweetie," he says, looking her straight in the eyes, "I want to talk about forgiving with you."

"I know," Emily says. "But it's easier said than done."

"I know," he says, tucking a strand of hair behind her ear. "Trust me, I know."

★ ★ ★

"So... they're building a school," Star says as she sits down at her desk. The tiny office is in the basement of yet another abandoned building in the middle of another city. No one's noticed, no one comes to this area except for druggies and homeless people, and they couldn't care less about what happens in the building.

"Yeah," he says, playing with a Rubik's cube. She's not sure where he got it from, but she really doesn't think it matters. "I don't feel right, Star," he says abruptly.

"About what, honey?" she asks.

"About taking their abilities. I thought you said we were making people better, not worse."

"But aren't there some people we don't want in our new

world, honey? People that are so willing to share secrets shouldn't be trusted with ours, right?"

"But they were just kids," he says, still staring at the Rubik's cube. She knows he won't look at her, not when they're arguing. If he looks at her he'll feel guilty and start apologizing. "I like kids. We're helping kids, right?"

"Not all kids," she says.

"But--"

"Why don't you go check on the pretty lady, honey? Make sure she seems comfortable," Star says.

"Yeah, okay," he says quietly, getting to his feet and heading for the stairs. She frowns slightly, thinking about how to deal with her partner thinking for himself.

CHAPTER SEVEN

"Think I should wear this or this?" Emily asks, barging into my room with Ditto in tow. They're wearing two different outfits, I notice as I glance over. But they're both wearing jeans and t-shirts, just different colors and pictures on the front. "Or should I put this shirt with those jeans?" she asks.

"Does it matter?" I ask, "the only people that are going to be there are the usual crowd--"

"And Cub!" she says as Ditto poofs out of existence. "Another girl, Trent! You don't think she'll pick on me, do you?" she asks as abruptly worried as she was excited. "She looked really tough."

"She can probably beat you," I say honestly. She's caught me in the middle of working out, but she doesn't seem to care that I'm doing sit-ups, so I just keep doing them--it's only when I start doing push-ups that she sits down on my back. "What are you doing?" I ask.

"Adding weight," she says. "You're getting flabby."

"Whatever," I mutter, flushing slightly. "Look, Cub's a super villain in training, right? You can't just assume that they're all like Max, got it? So be careful around her."

"I know," she says. "Oh! You're going to be on the news tonight, right? We should go see it!"

"Why? You saw it first hand," I say.

"But you're going to be *on TV*," she repeats, as if it's important. Dad and Mom are on television every once in a while, like, once a month practically. It makes me look like a total noob when I'm excited to see myself--

"Trent! Emily! Get in here! Everyone else is already here waiting!" Mom yells.

"Did you set it to record?" I hear Dad ask. "We've already got the Hero TV version--"

"Of course I set it to record!" Mom says.

"Trent! Hurry up already!" Max calls. "Flirting can wait!"

"We're coming!" Emily says, hopping off my back and racing into the front room. I get to my feet and follow at a slower pace.

"Would you hurry up already?" Emily demands. She's already sitting on the floor in front of the couch, waiting for me. I drop down next to her and lean against Dad's leg, since he's sitting behind me.

"And today had a bit of Super excitement," a lady says into the mic. "Maximum showed up right off the highway, only to have a newcomer stand up to him!" The screen changes, showing me throwing the bus at Max in a dramatic fashion. "We've done some research and it seems that the newcomer is none other than America's Son and Star Spangled's boy, Kid Liberty!"

The video changes, showing me crouching down and talking to the little boy. Somehow they even managed to capture the conversation, I think in amazement. "I'm here with the little boy that met Kid Liberty earlier," she goes one as the screen returns to her. The little black boy is standing next to her, beaming like he won the lottery. "You talked with Kid Liberty, right?" she says.

"Yes," the little boy rasps out.

"Did he seem nice?" she asks.

"He asked me if I'm going to be good," the boy says.

"I saw that!" she replies. "And what did you say?"

"I said yes," the boy says seriously.

"And how old are you?" she asks.

"I'm five and a half."

"I bet you're going to tell all your friends at kindergarten about this, right?" she says. I'm pretty sure she's realized she's getting nowhere, but he's too cute to mind that. The little boy nods enthusiastically. There's a crowd of people behind her, waving at the camera and trying to get some screen time. "What about you?" she asks an older girl. "Did you see the fight?"

"I did! He got hit with a bus," she says. "It was awesome!"

"So tell me, are you a new Kid Liberty fan?" the interviewer asks.

"Sure! But I felt a little sorry for Maximum, though. He got hit in the face."

"So you like Maximum?" the interviewer asks.

"Well, I mean, he was on YouTube and he stopped this crazy

kid not that long ago--I think he's just misunderstood."

"Because he's too cute to be really evil," another girl butts in.

"He seriously is!" the first girl agrees. "Oh, but that Kid Liberty was cute, too, wasn't he?"

"I think Maximum's just a little bit cuter, though."

"Either way it looks like we've got some up and coming capes to keep track of!" the interviewer says. "This is Renee, signing out." The show goes back to the two people at the desk, who are grinning.

"So you can't be really evil if you're cute, huh?" the man asks. "That's good to know."

"It's so good to see a new generation of old fashioned heroes," the woman says. "I'm a big fan of America's Son, myself, and his son looks so much like him!"

"That's funny, I'm a huge fan of Star Spangled," the man says. "That family is one to watch. Now, on a less super note--" The news becomes a drone in the background as the group starts to cheer.

"Ha! I'm cuter!" Max says, looking far too proud over that fact.

"They just didn't get a good enough shot of me," I say. "That or the girl was blind!"

"Very nice cover for your first fight," Dad says, messing up my short hair. "A feel good piece, sure, but since nothing major was destroyed it would be."

Emily's staring at me with a frown. I look at her. "What?" I ask.

"I'm trying to decide whether she was blind or not," she says seriously. I start tickling her.

"Admit she was blind," I say as she starts giggling.

"Stop! Stop!" she cries.

"Once you admit she's blind!"

"NEVER!" she says, trying to get free. "Okay fine! Someone's blind!" she says. I grin, pulling away. "You, that is," she says. Dad grabs me before I grab her again, and she hops up into my Mom's lap, sticking her tongue out at me.

"That's enough," Dad says with amusement. "Now, we're

going to discuss proper interview behavior as capes. Emily, you aren't in uniform yet, but you should listen. Firstly, whether you're the good guy or the bad, you've got little kids hanging on your every word. You do not curse. You can get creative all you want, but I don't want to hear some six year old cursing and saying they learned it from a Hall member, got it?"

"Sir, yes, sir," Max says.

"I'm holding you to it," Dad says. "I know some supers might not agree with me, but I don't care. They'll just beep the words out on news, anyway, so it's a waste of air time as well as offensive. You're free to give each other a hard time on television, though, but keep it superficial until you've been fighting for a while. They don't need to know that you two know each other well."

Emily slides back down to the ground, leaning back against Mom's legs.

"But I can make fun of his height, right?" I say.

"Of course," Dad says.

"Yeah? Well I can make fun of your empty head," Max mutters, throwing a couch pillow at me. I grab it and stick it behind me.

"My head's not empty!" I protest. "I'm thinking something right now!"

"What are you thinking?" he asks.

"Shorty, shorty, shorty--" I say, making Zoe have to grab Max from lunging at me.

"No fighting in the apartment building," she says, tugging him back onto the couch. "Dad'd kill you both then make you rebuild it."

"Where is your dad, anyway?" Max asks.

"He went out to check the school's security system again," Zoe says. "Ever since the sisters were caught he's been rebuilding it so that his brother won't be able to affect it."

"I think I'll take a quick walk," Dad says, getting up.

"Are you worried about him?" Mom asks.

"No, of course not. He's the son of Superior. I just feel like getting some air," Dad says. He's out the door the next second, leaving us to look at each other.

"He's worried," I say.

"Extremely," Mom agrees.

Nico goes perfectly still, the hairs on the back of his neck rising as he slowly turns. He'd sensed him coming, he thinks, he'd thought he'd been ready for the world warping, too--but it is a bit off-setting, even with expecting it.

"Hi," the man in front of him says, raising a hand. "So you're that girl's dad, right?" It's like looking in a mirror, in some ways, Nico notices. But just like the world all around him being the wrong colors, so is the man in front of him.

"And you're my brother," Nico says, "or something like that." Because there's something wrong with those pale gray eyes, he realizes. Something missing that he usually sees in his mirror, cynicism, maybe.

"We're family?" the man asks. "Oh, but I can't stay long," he goes one before Nico can respond. "I'm here to say sorry."

"What for?" Nico asks.

"We're trying to make the world better," the man says. "But she made it worse for those two. I'm sorry." He stops, looking up as if seeing something coming. "I've gotta go. Goodbye, brother," he says.

The world twists in on itself, jerking out from under Nico and flinging him backwards--and the negative him is gone. "Nico!" he hears, from a distance. "Nico, are you okay?" Ken appears in front of him, looking worried. "What just happened?" he demands.

"I met my brother," Nico says, shaking his head and shoving himself to his feet, "I think."

"Did he hurt you?" Ken asks.

"No. He apologized," Nico says, his confusion showing. "Ken... it was like talking with a kid. Not one of our kids--a *little* kid."

"What?"

"Exactly."

★ ★ ★

"Wake up! Wake up, wake up, wake up!" I wake up. Hard not to when a ninety-something pound ball of energy jumps on top of you. She's got me pinned under the blankets, but doesn't seem to care. I look at her sleepily.

"What?" I ask.

"It's school!" she says. "Get up and get dressed, we gotta get to school!"

"Emily, honey, quit assaulting Trent and come get your breakfast!" Mom calls from the kitchen.

"Coming!" Emily calls back. "If you don't hurry I'm going to eat yours, too," she threatens before racing off.

"Don't let her eat mine!" I call from my room before heading for my shower. I come out a few minutes later, get dressed, and head into the kitchen to sit down across from Emily. "You're *way* too excited for school," I say.

"Like you aren't," she says. "Think of it, a school where you don't have to hide what you can do at all! I can make Ditto take notes for me! I can run as fast as I want in gym, it's--it's like a dream." Her eyes are shiny and her smile's so wide that my cheeks hurt just looking at it.

"Okay, okay," I say as I start eating my rather large breakfast, finishing off my plate quickly. I stand up when I'm finished, kiss my mother on the cheek, and grab my bag, leaving Emily to shove the last bit of food into her mouth and chase after me. She's still chewing as we start down the stairs--and Sunny falls on me from behind.

I jerk, looking at him blankly as his head rests on my shoulder. He snores in my ear. "You can carry him!" Zoe says, going past me and falling into step with Emily. "Otherwise he's never going to get there in time!"

"Oh for crying out loud," I mutter, not even that surprised when Sunny wakes up just enough to climb onto my back, piggyback style. "You owe me, man," I mutter, starting down the stairs again. The funniest part, though, is that Nico's sauntering along behind us with a cup of coffee in his hand as if he's got all the time in the world. "I thought principals were supposed to be the first ones there," I say over my shoulder.

"Eh, it goes against my super villain nature to be on time for anything," he says. "Also, you realize he's going to do that to you every morning, don't you?"

"I'm trying to ignore that fact," I admit as we reach the bottom of the stairs and get in line to exit the security system. "Hey--hey SUNNY!" I yell in his ear. "You gotta go through the security system, man!"

"Five more minutes," Sunny mumbles.

"There's something really wrong about carrying another guy piggyback," I complain as I drop him on his butt--or try to. He's got a good hold on my neck and doesn't seem to be letting go anytime soon. "Sunny!" I say. "Get off, you gotta do this on your own!"

"Want to borrow the blow horn?" Nico asks.

"Please," I say, plugging my ears with my fingers as Nico brings out the blow horn--and blows it right in Sunny's ears. "Although it'll be your fault if he goes deaf," I add as Sunny yelps and wakes up.

"I'm up, I'm up! Sheesh," he mutters, stumbling over to the door and pressing his hand against the screen. "That's got to be child abuse," he mutters.

I follow, pressing my hand and exiting the building when it's my turn. Once outside, though, I look around cautiously. "They know where we live," I say to Nico.

"Yeah," he says. "Which is why we've got the entire staff of semi-retired hero teachers hovering over our heads right now."

I see them, now that he's mentioned it. "Is that Banshee?" I ask, pointing at a rather dangerous looking woman with long brown hair. "I heard she was working overseas."

"She's the music teacher."

"Seriously?" I say.

"According to Double M himself," Nico says, taking another drink of coffee. "I'm not sure my kids can carry a note in a bucket--I know Zoe can't, haven't heard Sunny try, but Double M insists."

"That's Taurus," I say, my eyes catching on a huge Minotaur man sitting on another roof.

"He's the gym teacher," Nico says. "That's why he's the only fully acting hero we've got. He'll be joining Central Hall, too."

There are others, I notice, about six in total, all names and faces that I recognize straight off--we're talking the big names of the past few centuries, ones that have done their civic duty a million times over and survived. I'm not going to lie, I'm a bit speechless. And Mom and Liz aren't even here yet--I think they're going to show up when Nico decides when their class will be.

"You can close your mouth," Nico says. "One of the major reasons they're so willing to sign up was because they're ready to take me down if need be."

"Could they?" I ask.

"Together? Absolutely," Nico says. "Doesn't matter, I've got enough on my hands to deal with. So, first day of school with your cute little girlfriend, huh?"

"What?" I ask, jerking. I just passed Sunny--who's half asleep on his feet, soaking up the sun again. I'm tempted to go in a large circle around him, but I'm too late. He grabs me.

"Carry me," he says dramatically, wrapping his arms around my chest from behind and dragging along behind me.

"Oh for pete's sake," I mutter, stopping. "Get offa me you lazy punk, otherwise we'll both be tardy." Unfortunately he seems to have misinterpreted what I just said, because he's climbing onto my back again. "No--no--this is definitely not how a super hero goes to school on the first day!" I protest, trying to get him off. It's like trying to remove a superpowered vine. Once I move one arm it latches on somewhere else.

"Are you two dating?" Emily asks, looking back at me.

"No! Absolutely not!" I say, absolutely appalled at that question. "I like--" can't say "you" in this situation, can I? "girls! He's just a friend! He's--he's--I'm going to kill you, Sunny," I mutter as she snaps a picture of us with her cellphone.

Sunny snores again. But that's not nearly as embarrassing as the sound of the supers above us laughing. "He's solar powered!" I call up to them. "Stupid elementalist." And that just makes them laugh harder. "Zoe, he's your brother, you carry him!" I call to Zoe.

"Heck no, I don't care if he's tardy!" she calls back. "Just drop him on the concrete, he'll wake up in a few hours!"

Nico is laughing. "Nico, he's your kid! You carry him!" I call out.

"I agree with Zoe!" he says. "But I might give you both detention if he's tardy too many times, so think it through!"

"Why would I get detention?" I demand, reluctantly carrying the sleeping plant boy to the school.

"Because you're a working hero now, Trent! Saving people is part of the job--so save Sunny from detention!"

"Oh for crying out loud," I complain and keep walking. I can't help scanning the sky, though, wondering if someone or something is going to happen--but I should have been looking at the school.

A poof of smoke appears right in front of Death Canyon and dramatic laughter echoes in my ears. The supers above all turn, ready to fight as a large black man in a dramatic African outfit appears, holding a staff in his hand. "Heroes of Central Hall," he proclaims in a voice that carries. "I have come!"

"Panther, you dare to--" Banshee starts out, only to stop as Nico raises a hand.

"This one's mine!" Nico calls up to them, still holding his coffee cup as he saunters lazily towards one of the most famous super villains around. For a moment it almost looks dramatic--then Panther lets out a laugh of joy.

"Nico! My old friend, when did you get out?" he asks, throwing his arms around Nico in a hug. Nico starts laughing, hugging the big man back and pounding him on the back.

"Not too long ago--I've been busy or I would have called, honestly," he says, pulling back with a wide grin. "How's Amara?"

"She is well, as beautiful as ever--and twice as demanding," Panther says dryly, grinning from ear to ear. "Are you involved in this school?"

"I'm the principal," Nico says. "I heard your girl's going to be joining us, right? Is she as pretty as your wife?"

"She is her spitting image at that age," Panther says, turning to the silent teenager that I hadn't even noticed until now. "Adanna, come, meet my old friend," he says. She's tall for a fourteen year old girl, as tall as Max, at least, and thin. She's wearing a baseball hat and baggy clothes, but she moves like a dancer. If she's trying to hide the fact that she's a girl, she's failing.

"Sunny," I say.

"Five more minutes," he mumbles.

"Sunny, you really need to wake up," I hiss. "Seriously need to wake up--not even kidding here."

"Huh?" he says, managing to open his eyes.

"Remove the hat, Adanna," Black Panther says. The girl reluctantly tugs off her baseball hat, revealing her black hair is braided tight against her skull and stops at the top of her neck, and her face--she looks like a model. That's the face you see on those teen magazines aimed at girls in line at the super market. Her eyes are yellow gold in color, a striking contrast to her dark brown skin.

"Holy crap," Sunny says.

Not the most eloquent of reactions, but I totally get where he's coming from.

"Zoe, get over here, kiddo. Sunny, you too," Nico calls. Sunny hops off my back and heads forward, completely awake by now. It figures that a pretty face would do it, I think with amusement. "Pan, Adanna, meet my twins, Zoe and Sunny," he says, dropping a hand on each of their shoulders.

"Hi," Sunny says, holding out his hand.

"You look very much like your father," Pan says as he takes the hand. "Is your power the same?"

"No, he takes after his mom," Nico says. "Zoe here takes after me."

"I see," Panther says. "And your powers are, Sunny?"

"Plants, and maybe earth, I guess?" Sunny says, covering a yawn with his free hand. "I'm an elementalist."

There's a look of surprise on Panther's face, mixed with a hint of wonder as he lets go. He looks at Nico. "So you have both a technopath and an elementalist child?" he says quietly. "Will they become villains?"

"It's up to them," Nico says. "But honestly I'm trying to talk Zoe into it and Sunny out of it."

"I see! You will make a wonderful super villain," Panther says, shaking Zoe's hands. "Your father was a true credit to our side." Is it just me or does he seem relieved at that statement? Maybe the idea of an elementalist as a super villain is even off-putting to super villains. I know it scares me. Thankfully, Sunny's too lazy to get into the whole "causing havoc for havoc's sake" sort of thing.

"Um... thanks, I think?" Zoe says.

Sunny's taken advantage of this and moved towards Adanna, his hand held out and a grin on his face. "Hi, I'm Sunny," he says.

She looks at him, not offering her hand. "You are lazy," she says coldly. "You should walk to school on your own power or not come at all. You are not fit to be a proper super villain."

Ouch. Doesn't help that she's taller than him, either, I notice, poor guy.

"That's fine, I'm not going to be one," Sunny says, letting his hand drop. He looks around, and then heads back to where I'm standing, discreetly elbowing me in the gut. "Thanks for waking me up," he drawls sarcastically.

"Hey, she's got a point," I admit. "You're lazy in the mornings." Even as I say that he's tilting his head back and closing his eyes as he holds out his arms, soaking up the early morning sun again. After a second he growls something incomprehensible and tugs his t-shirt off, revealing a thin white tank top.

"I dunno why, but I think I'm not getting enough sun, or something," Sunny says. "It's weird."

I glance up as Max pulls to a stop behind us, wearing civvies. "What I miss?" he asks me, glancing around. "Hey, is that Banshee?"

"Black Panther and his daughter showed up," I say, nodding in their direction. "And the daughter shot Sunny down straight off, told him he's too lazy to be a super villain."

"He is," Max says, looking at her, and then looking at Sunny doing his sun thing. "Is it just me or does him doing that make you nervous?" he asks quietly. "Why'd he take his shirt off?"

"I'm pretty sure I'm right about him being solar powered," I admit. "More than likely he's going to start getting taller pretty quick, or something."

"Like a plant," Max says dryly.

"You laugh, but I'll lay odds on it," I say. "Maybe you should stand in the sun more often."

"Ha ha," he says. "Very funny."

"I thought so!" I say.

Zoe steps forward, offering her hand to Cub at this point, so I stop joking and listen in intently. "Hi," she says. "I'm Zoe."

"I am Cu--Adanna," Adanna says, shaking the hand that's offered. "It is good to meet a fellow villain."

"Well, I actually haven't decided yet," Zoe admits. "Does dating one count?"

"That's my cue," Max says, heading for the two girls. I'm actually not that surprised as Emily takes his place, standing close to me with a worried expression on her face.

"What's wrong?" I ask, dropping an arm over her shoulders. She leans in unconsciously, a sure sign that she's not paying attention.

"I don't think she's going to like me," she whispers, looking as if the world has already crashed around her.

"Hey, you don't know that for sure," I whisper back.

"But I'm not going to be a villain," she says. "You aren't, either. So she won't like either of us, right?" Adanna is looking past Max and straight at us, and I realize that there's a very good chance she's listening to everything we say.

"Maybe," I admit. "But just because they're on the same side doesn't mean they've got to like each other in their private lives, right? And just because they're on the opposite side doesn't mean they've got to dislike each other in their private lives, either. You just be you," I tell her. "No point in worrying about the rest of it."

She nods, but the way she's being clingy tells me she doesn't really believe it. The heroes are landing all around us, talking among themselves. Taurus, though, heads straight for me as he shifts into his human form. As a human he's a tough looking black man with a short cut goatee and long dreadlocks pulled up in a ponytail--his Minotaur form is three times larger, but his human form is as big as my Dad is. "I'm thinking that you're Kid Liberty?" he offers.

"You're right," I say with a grin, taking the offered hand. "Trent Styles. This is my future partner, Emily Dreyton," I add. "Emily, this is Taurus, one of the heaviest hitters out there, in his shifted form. Dad's a big fan of his, he's got at least three of his T-shirts."

"America's Son is a fan of mine?" Taurus asks. "I'm honored." He offers Emily his hand, who takes it shyly. "It's a pleasure to meet a future Liberty girl," Taurus adds, grinning at her.

"Thank you," she says.

"Is it too early to ask your abilities?" Taurus asks. Ditto poofs into existence on my right side, rather than Emily trying to explain. The startled look on Taurus's face changes to a laugh as he looks at her. "A duplicator! I never thought I'd get to meet one," he says, shaking Ditto's hand as well.

We've got a crowd by this time, since the heroes all want to talk about the fight from yesterday or examine Ditto curiously. The more people that approach her, though, the closer Emily and Ditto move to me. They're practically hiding under my arms by the time Nico whistles loudly.

"It's time to offend all the heroes!" he says cheerfully. "So if you'd line up I'll scan you and input you into the security system, otherwise you won't be able to enter--at least in one piece."

"Really, did he have to put it that way?" Taurus asks me.

"It's one of the perks of the job," Nico calls over to him. "But I promise not to tell what classes you're all ranked as--although we all know they're either A or the rare S class since Double M handpicked you, so really it's not that big of a threat. Shame, that. Panther, I'm afraid I can't allow you access--you know that, though."

"I'd be offended if I was trusted enough for that," Panther says. "But if it were anyone other than you, there would be problems."

"Of course," Nico says. "Why don't you and the family come over for a barbecue sometime? You can meet the rest of the gang."

"I'd be happy to." He turns, pulling Cub forward. "Adanna, you will train under these people. You will learn how heroes operate, and you will learn how to be a better super villain because of it," he says.

"Yes, Papa," Cub says. She blushes as he pats her on the shoulder before taking off at full speed. For a second there's a slightly panicked look on her face as the heroes move past her, and she takes a step back. I can practically hear her thoughts. She's completely surrounded by the enemy, and not just any enemy, enemies that all outclass her by a mile.

Emily and Ditto are watching her like Siamese cats watching a toy. I wonder if they even realize it.

"Why don't you go introduce yourself?" I say to them.

"But--" they say, both looking at me. "You come too," they say, grabbing my arms and tugging me forward. "Hi," they say, the same tone, same expression, everything. "I'm Emily."

"There are two of you," Cub says. "Why do you say 'I'?"

"This one's Ditto," I say, raising my right arm and her holding hands with it. "Emily's a duplicator."

"I see," Cub says, watching Ditto closely, and then watching Emily just as closely. "I am Cu--Adanna."

"Cub, right?" I say. "I'm Trent," I add, offering my hand.

"I no longer have claim to that title," she says. "It belongs to my brother."

"When you're growing out of it, he'll be growing into it," Nico says. "If you want to be called Cub here, we don't mind."

"No, I can't," she says. "I am Adanna. I will be called Adanna." She looks at me. "You are both heroes?" she asks, looking to Emily as well.

"Yeah, we are," I say.

"Then we are at odds."

"Do we have to be?" Emily asks.

"Yes," Cu--Adanna says, "we do."

Well there goes Emily's hope. This girl's really good at shooting people down, isn't she?

★ ★ ★

"Welcome to Cape High," Nico says as we all step onto the campus grounds. "I think this is a better place to introduce ourselves--for now we have a pretty small class, so we'll start with them. First, my kids, Sunny and Zoe," he says. Zoe raises a hand and Sunny glances up from where he's back to sunbathing. "Zoe is a technopath--or will be once she gains some control, Sunny's an earth elementalist. Next are our two poster boys, Max and Trent-- you all saw them yesterday on Hero TV. Max specializes in gravity, Trent is a tank. And our last two are the newcomers to the group, Emily and Adanna. Emily, as you saw earlier is a duplicator, Adanna is a shapeshifter, right?"

"Yes," Adanna says.

"And as most of you have been informed, we have a slight problem in the area," Nico goes on. "Which is why I'm going to ask you to bear with me, Adanna, when I say I'd like you to have an escort back and forth from school. I can do it, if you want, or we can have one of the supers that live in the same direction as you do meet up with you."

"No," she says. "I am a super villain--"

"Right now you're just a kid," Nico interrupts. "What side you choose in the future is just that--in the future. At this moment you are a student of the school, and we will keep you safe. If any of you teachers disagree with this I'd like for you to speak up now so we can find a replacement. I won't have the prospective villains treated any different from the prospective heroes, do I make myself clear?"

"If they break the rules, I expect them to be punished for it," Banshee says, "regardless of what side their family is on."

"That's perfectly acceptable," Nico says.

"We do have the right to try and persuade the kids towards heroism, though, right?" Taurus asks.

"Persuade, maybe, shove it down their throat, not at all," Nico says. "I actually think that should be something the kids decide for themselves. But we will make sure they learn proper cape protocol--I don't want any of them winding up in the Cape Cells."

"Why don't we go straight to the matter," Mega says abruptly. I'm surprised he's been quiet up until now. "Technico is an ex super villain. We all realize it. That means he's biased towards super villains, his kids will become super villains, his grandkids--"

"No they won't," Nico says, startling Mega. "I wouldn't mind if Zoe did, honestly, but Sunny probably won't, no matter what someone else says. Will you, Sunny?"

"Nope, even though it might be entertaining," Sunny says, looking up from his sunbathing. "I decided earlier."

"And what will you do, be a hero?" Mega asks curiously.

"Well, in a way," Sunny says.

"He is taking this far too lightly," Adanna says sharply. "It is an honor to continue your family's position in the super world."

"Oh, he will be," Nico says, "just not mine. But regardless of your personal choices we aren't here to pick and choose who gets taught better than another. I'm here to make sure that each student learns to be the best super they can be. I hope the rest of you are here for the same reason."

Sunny flops down on his back without even bending his knees, resting his head on his hands and letting out a happy sigh as the sun hits him straight on. The rest of the group just stare at him for a long moment before Mega asks, a bit hesitantly, "Is there something wrong with that boy?"

"He's solar powered," I volunteer. "He needs to charge up." Max starts laughing. "I swear he's getting stranger by the day, though," I admit, walking over and crouching down next to Sunny. "Hey--hey, Sunny, wake up, man." Sleepy green eyes open, looking at me.

"I've already had the tour," he says. "Wake me up when you're back."

"Alright," I say, standing. "He says he's going to skip the tour."

"That is--" Mega starts out.

"Fine," Nico says. "It's either we leave him here or someone carries him anyway," he adds. "Now if you would all follow me--"

I glance back at Sunny, wondering if leaving him in contact with the ground like this is smart, considering. But if he's asleep nothing can really happen, right? With that thought I shrug and follow the rest of the group.

Several miles up, hiding among the clouds, the white haired man floats, watching the scene below. It took a little bit of staring, but he can see through the strange bubble that hides it now. It's a school. He's read about schools. They sound like a lot of fun to him. But he's been close to that school before, and he got shot for it. It stung a lot, and even did some damage to his arm, so he can't go.

Instead he just floats there, watching the boy lying on the ground in front of the buildings. There's something about that boy, he thinks, something fascinating. Just as he decides that, the earth under the boy lurches upwards, lifting him up and cradling him in an oval shaped bed. Tiny flowers sprout from the dirt bed, surrounding the boy.

The man laughs in wonder. Yes, he thinks, this is what the world should be like! He needs to convince Star that more people need powers like this so everyone can sleep so perfectly! He flies off at top speed, leaving the school behind to go do just that.

CHAPTER EIGHT

We make it back to the front of the campus about half an hour later, and I can't help but stare at the bed that's built itself for the still sleeping Sunny. Thing is, I'm the least reactive of the group. The supers themselves are crowded around the bed, poking the construction as if something other than dirt and rock is there.

"What?" Sunny mutters, yawning hugely as he sits up. He almost falls out of the bed. "Wh--what the--" It collapses underneath him, dropping him on the ground. "Whoa, wasn't expecting that," he says.

"Good to see you're finally awake," Nico says. "Get up, it's time to do the course planning."

"Yeah, yeah I'm coming," Sunny says, standing up and dusting his pants off. He stretches his arms over his head with another yawn. "That was a great sleep, though," he says. "Hey, Trent! Did you carry me this morning?"

"Unfortunately," I say, wondering why he's so cheerful now. You know how I said he was solar powered? I'm positive he is, now. Not a doubt in my mind about it.

"Thanks!"

"And it's decided, Sunny's first hour is a nap in the sun," Nico says dryly. "This is the first time I've seen him this awake since... ever."

"Isn't he your son?" Mega asks.

"Yeah, but he doesn't tend to take naps outside. Usually he sleeps in until we use the blow horn. But thinking of it, I'm not that surprised."

"How is a nap part of a training process?" Mega demands. "Let him sleep in the sun on his own time."

"Do you want to borrow the blow horn for every class you've got him for?" Nico asks. "Because I don't know about you, but my hearing is too good to have to put up with it that often. Once a day is about all I can handle, honestly."

"Fine, and what about the others? How do you suppose we train them while keeping their education levels high?" Mega asks as we head into the dirt area of the second building. Nico heads to the side of the room and pulls a machine out of the wall, motioning me forward.

"Trent, you're the most rounded, I'd say, so come here for a bit," he says. I have to weave through the crowd but I make it to the front quickly enough. He starts taping small suction cups to my skin, arms, under my shirt, forehead, even my legs, and then starts typing on the computer attached to the suction cups by wires. "Let's see..."

I peek over his shoulder, seeing a line drawing of a male that's color coordinated to indicate certain things--it's mostly red, and obviously me. He taps a few buttons and brings up a chart listing several things, such as muscle strength, flexibility, denseness, and other.

"What's the other?" I ask.

"I'm not sure," Nico says, tapping on the word. "Huh... a touch of empathy," he says. "Not much, which doesn't surprise me, considering, but I wasn't expecting it at all."

"And how did you get all this information on abilities?" Mega asks, looking at the screen as well.

"I hacked into the Hall during my time in the Cape Cells," Nico admits shamelessly. "I've had it on mental record for years, so I figured I might as well use it for the school project. Certain tells are present in the muscle and brain wave structure of each super--if you see similar tells in the kids, there's a good chance they've got the same. We've got information from generations worth of supers, after all, the database is huge. Nobody was doing anything with it, though."

"And how did you hack the records when you were never given access to a computer?" Mega asks.

"Mega, haven't you realized?" Nico says, starting to pull the tabs off of me. "My brain *is* a computer. Max, you're next!"

"What does it mean, though?" I ask. "I'm an empath?"

"Just enough to unconsciously pick up on emotions, not much more than a dog, really," Nico says bluntly. "You won't be able to do much with it--except, considering you're a hero, talk people down from tall heights, maybe. Other than that, well, it's pretty useless. We can develop it more if you want, but it'll never be something you can call a proper ability."

Max is putting the tabs on himself, distracting Nico from our conversation. "Can you tell IQ with this?" Max asks.

"Only if the enhanced IQ is super power related," Nico says, letting him do the work for him. I'm curious, so I stick around to see his outline. There's a decent amount of red, but the majority of the color is light blue. There are a few lines of yellow, as well. I have no clue what that means other than he's got enhanced strength. I'm guessing the blue indicates his gravity powers in some way. "Yeah, I expected this, too," Nico says.

"What?"

"You've got your Dad's telekineses--I'm thinking it manifests in your gravity powers, and you've got latent telepathy."

"Seriously?" Max asks. "But I could never get it to work! I've tried!"

"Most likely your instinctive shields are too strong. We'll work on it," Nico says. "Emily, you're next, kid," he says. "I'm looking forward to this one, honestly, I've only got a bit of information on creation types. You're almost as rare as an elementalist in your own way."

She nods and goes forward, helping put the tabs on and looking at Nico expectantly as he brings her up on the screen. He stares at it, taps on the keyboard a few times, and then looks at her. "Some of this I expected," he says after a second. "But you're a telepath--then again, I expect the two versions of you do communicate well, so it makes sense. You've got decent strength but nothing near the boys', speed is C class... extreme healing abilities, like you said. It's the creation lines that fascinate me--the levels are close to A class. Have you tried creating anything other than Ditto?"

"No, but I'd like to," she says.

"We'll work on it."

"Okay," she says, grinning wickedly. I can only imagine what she'll make when she can.

"Adanna," Nico says, motioning her forward. He doesn't say anything about her abilities, only reaches up and pats her on the back. "Sunny," he says. Sunny saunters forward, walking right past Adanna, ignoring her totally, and starts putting the tabs on. Nico moves every single one he puts on. "You weren't paying attention, were you?" Nico asks.

Sunny pokes the one on his forehead curiously. "So what's this going to tell you about me, anyway?"

"Not sure," Nico admits. "I've only got a few elementalists on record." He starts typing, bringing up Sunny's form. A long whistle escapes him.

"And your findings?" Mega asks.

"He's strong," Nico says. "Honestly, as far as I can tell, he's in the middle of a power growth spurt. I expected it somewhat, considering his age, but this is... I'm not sure I can graph it until it stablizes. I'll have to do this over a time period and compare the results to even have a clue where to start. Now..." He lets out a sigh, looking at Zoe. "Zoe, honey, I want you to be extremely calm--does anyone have something she can read?"

Taurus steps forward, handing over a sports magazine. Zoe takes it, not looking too enthusiastic, and starts flipping through it as Nico attaches the tabs. "Everyone step back," Nico drawls.

We all step back as he starts typing. Then he curses, groaning as the digital representation of her on the screen starts looking around. "Hey," it says, "what just happened?"

I look at Zoe, but she's gone perfectly still, her eyes look lifeless.

"She hijacked it," Nico says. "Zoe, can you hear me?" he asks the computer.

"Yeah, I can hear you. Dad where am I?" she asks from inside the computer. "Wow, there's a lot of interesting stuff in here! Oh, wait, I'm not exploding the computer! Dad, I'm not exploding the computer!" The avatar is jumping around like a cheerleader. "Hey, can I get on the net from here?"

"NO!" Nico yells.

"Darn it," she pouts.

"Well while you're in there hold perfectly still for a second, would you?" Nico says. "I want to take your specs."

"Okay."

He starts typing, as if having his daughter in a computer is a mere hindrance rather than a terrifying experience. Maybe for him it is, I realize. "Turn around, kiddo, I might as well take advantage of the situation," he says. The avatar turns around and he nods, bringing up her charts. She peeks around the window with her charts on them, looking at them curiously.

"Looks like you're growing at the same rate as your brother," he says. "Now out! Focus on your physical body."

"Can't I play some games first?" she asks. "You've got a couple on here!"

"Maybe later, now out of my computer."

"Okay, okay," she says. A second later her eyes change and she blinks, looking around. "That was pretty cool," she says.

"It scared the crap out of me," Max mutters. He's right next to her. "You're all the way back, right?"

"Yeah, think so," she says. "Relax, it didn't blow up!" she brags.

"Yeah, yeah," Max says, wrapping an arm around her waist. "Warn me before you do that again."

"Sure, but it's not like I knew I was going to do it ahead of time," she says. "He's got games," she adds. "I think he's been in it himself."

"Makes sense, it's like the ultimate digital reality game, right?"

"Yesss," she says.

"Looks like Zoe's got a new hobby," I say.

"Actually," Nico says, "we'll make that your first hour class. For everyone we'll go specialized for first and last hour, we have enough teachers. Then we'll have the basics, math, English, mad science, lunch, then go into history--"

"Science," Mega says. "Not mad science, just science."

"Where's the fun in that?" Nico asks. "Actually you guys can figure out the middle hours yourselves. I expect you all know enough about the subjects to make sure they know how to read and write by the time they graduate. But for first hour and after three, I want to set them up with their training. In the morning Sunny gets nap time, Zoe, game time, Adanna, you'll spend it in shifted form--"

"But--" Adanna says, looking worried. "It's--um--"

"You can choose to do so wherever you want, and do whatever you want, while shifted. And seeing as you're a shifter as well, Taurus, can you oversee her training?"

"Yeah, I can do that," Taurus says.

Emily, you'll spend the first hour trying to create people other than Ditto," Nico says. "Pranks are perfectly acceptable--if you can get someone else blamed, then you get a gold star."

"That is absolutely not accep--" Mega starts out, only to be drowned out as everyone else starts to laugh.

"No hurting people, of course, and no slitting clothes, okay?" Nico says.

"Okay!" Emily says excitedly.

"I'd like for you all--both students and teachers--to help her out with this," Nico adds. "She's going to need help observing ways of moving, talking, walking, everything. Max, Trent? You two will be sparring on the field," he says, looking to us. "Do it up, we'll bring in some buses, and other things to throw, but keep it on the field and controlled, understand?"

"Yeah, we get it," Max says, grinning widely.

"This schedule will last until I say it's time to move to the next stage," Nico says. "Probably a month or two for most of you."

"Hey, do we all get gold stars?" Emily asks. "What do we get to do with them?"

"Hmm... if you get enough gold stars we'll have an ice cream party or something," Nico declares. "Oh, and Trent, I still owe you a car."

"It can wait until things have calmed down," I say, shrugging. "So is the last hour the same?" I ask.

"No, for the last hour or more we'll start training on obstacle courses," Nico says. "Since Jeanie and Liz are so intent on teaching the girls girl power, or whatever, we'll toss some of that in once a week. We'll also bring in teamwork plays for you and Emily."

"And music?" Banshee asks.

"Zoe can't carry a note in a bucket, but if you want to teach them to sing I'm willing to let you suffer through it," Nico says. "Honestly I think you're here for a kid that Double M hasn't gotten yet, but maybe he knows something I don't."

"So he's planning on getting more kids?" she asks.

"Yeah. He's got one he says he wants from the west branch-- an orphan like Emily," I say.

"A guy," Sunny adds.

"I see," she says. "Then maybe musical instruments if anyone's interested."

"I'd like to learn the guitar!" I say.

"I want to do drums!" Sunny says.

"Do we have a bass? Any bass players here? I've almost got a band," Banshee says.

"I'll do it," Max says.

"Now we need a singer," she says. Her eyes fall on Adanna and Emily. "Can either of you sing?"

"Not a clue," Emily says.

"I would rather not," Adanna says.

"We'll have tryouts," Banshee says happily.

"Fine, and since it's a small group all around the same age," Nico says, "we'll stick them all in the same classes to begin with. Are we good?"

"Today was supposed to be the first day," Mega points out. "Shouldn't we do an actual class? Or several?"

"Sure. Kids, go do your self-studies, we'll let the teachers draw lots for what hour they get for their classes," Nico says.

"Sure," I say. "C'mon, Max, let's spar."

"I sortta want to watch Zoe--" Max starts out. I grab his arm, hauling him along behind him. "But digital Zoe," he says, "she's so cute--"

"Get over it," I say. "Good luck on your training, Em!" I call over my shoulder.

"You too!" she says, already heading out to find someplace to work.

"I don't want to sleep," I hear Sunny say. "Can I help Emily?"

"He's moving in on your girl, man," Max points out.

"And we're surprised by this?" I drawl. Spar or make sure Sunny doesn't get Emily... man that's a hard choice. "Nah, it takes more than just helping her out," I decide. "C'mon, let's do this quick."

"Sounds like a plan."

"You sent them off for more than just training, didn't you," Taurus says as the teachers gather around the table on the second floor of the experiment building. He looks straight at Nico. "Because you hauled me back before I could follow Panther's girl."

"Have you all heard what's going on in this area?" Nico asks. "I'll let you follow the kids after we go over this. First, Trent was going to a local school and his principal called him in--there was this woman in the room," he says, turning his laptop so they could see the thin woman. "He ran, we transferred him, and the next day the principal was found foaming at the mouth and with his mind mixed like a blender."

"There's more, isn't there?" Blackjack, a wiry super that specializes in illusion, says. "You wouldn't have built a security system ten times heavier than Cape Cells just because a norm was attacked." He's playing with a deck of cards as he says that, like he's not taking any of this very seriously, regardless.

"There's more. We had two small time super girls come for a tour of the school. They were escorted home and came back secretly because of a grudge against Emily, and were caught by this woman and a man that looks just like me." He turns the screen around, pushing play and letting them watch as the two girls were caught, grilled, and lost their abilities right in front of the school. "They lost their abilities. This man, at first I thought he was a sibling, now I'm not so sure."

"And why's that?" Taurus asks.

"Because he came to see me," Nico says. He looks at them each closely, as if testing their responses. "He speaks like a child. My daughter met him once before, but she was so distracted by his abilities that she didn't notice or didn't mention the simpleness."

"And what are his abilities?" Banshee asks.

"I don't know the extent," Nico says. "But he can cause my security cameras to go crazy--or he could at first. I think he can do the same to a man's mind. He's dangerous, sure, but her... if she can take powers away, she might be the one that tried to give powers to Jack."

"You're sure it's her, not him?" Taurus asks.

"I watched the video several times. She slips a needle into them. It's her."

"I see why you want Adanna to have an escort," Taurus says. "But you have to take into account her father. He's not going to be happy having a super hero walk his daughter home."

"That leaves me doing it," Nico says, "or Max."

"Max is still young--do you really think he can take on your... brother?" Blackjack asks.

"I'm not sure," Nico admits. "Of all the students he's the only one I'm trusting to fly here on his own--the others live in my apartment building--or are Adanna. But really, I can call a few friends in, nice respectable super villains that have a vested interest in this school, if Panther isn't willing to bring her himself."

"How would they have a vested interest in this?"

"Because they're watching right now to see how I train the super villains I have," Nico says. "You might not realize it, but most of the super villains are my age now, with kids the same age as mine. Just look at Pan. I can find them, I'm sure. I just need to make a few phone calls." He looks at them each. "Now I'm putting my trust in you," he says. "My kids, my friends' kids, these things are reliant on us. It goes beyond the game of good guys and bad guys that we used to play."

"Of course," Banshee says. "They're our future."

"We're heroes," Blackjack says. "Taking care of kids comes with the job description."

"Jack... he was the one on YouTube? What happened to him?" Taurus asks.

"I'm working on it," Nico says. "If I push too hard and too fast to get the metallic parts to retreat it rips into him. It's slow and a pain in the neck, put bluntly. What they've done to a norm is worse than abuse. But the fact that they can take powers away, as well-- we're dealing with a very dangerous pair."

"Call your friends," Mega says, making Nico jerk. "I don't have kids of my own," he goes on, "but I watched Trent grow up. I love that kid. I was worried when he started having trouble. When your kids and Max showed up, he turned back into the happy kid I think of as a nephew. Now he's got a future partner and a job as a hero, it's more than I can ask for, honestly. So I figure, even though I didn't want to at first, I'm going to throw my lot in with you. I'll trust your decisions, *to a point.*"

"It was the pranks for Emily that added that 'to a point' wasn't it?" Nico says.

"Of course it is! She's a future hero--a future Liberty! You're training her to be--"

"Oh let it go, Mega, a bit of honest trickery on the good side isn't going to be that big of a problem," Banshee says. "I bet that's part of why Trent picked her. He takes after his dad. You can't exactly sneak in when you're a walking tank. Some jobs require a bit of delicacy."

"Trent picked her because she's adorable and he's crushing hard," Nico says. "He used that excuse because she still hasn't figured out how bad he's got it. But it works, so we can't complain." He turns the laptop back to himself. "Now, since we've discussed the problem, I'll let you go see what the kids are doing."

"And you?" Mega asks.

"Oh, I've got this entire place wired," Nico says. "I can watch them all at once right where I'm at," he adds, kicking his feet up on the table and placing the laptop on his lap.

He'd been planning on helping Emily, Sunny thinks as he creeps closer to the back of the second building, so why is he stalking Adanna instead? Probably because he's seen Ditto before. He's never seen a shape shifter shift in person! Yeah, he thinks as he peeks around the corner, this is all about having a new exper--

A tiny black cub sits in the middle of the dirt, looking miserable. He can't help but fall forward onto his hands and knees at the sight. She's about the size of a house cat, and her fur is fluffy and sticking up in all directions. And, he thinks inevitably, she's looking straight at him.

"Um--uh--sorry? I got lost," he says, backing up with his hands in the air. The cub stands up, shakily, and straight leg struts a few steps before tumbling over her own paws. A tiny little mewing sound comes from her, which he's almost positive is cursing in kitty. "Hey, don't get mad," he says, crawling over to her. "I'm really new to my abilities too! I mean, I've been tripped by flowers more times than I can count!" His hand reaches out and pats her head--only to get bit by tiny teeth. "Hey, that hurts," he complains, tugging his hand away.

She lets go and hisses at him, her fur fluffing up more. "Okay, I get it, no petting," he says, looking at his hand. She didn't pierce the skin, thankfully, but it hadn't been fun! "I promise," he says, "no touching."

He looks away from her, not really wanting to leave but knowing she's not going to calm down with him staring at her. Absently he pokes the dirt with a finger, a bit surprised as the finger sinks into the hard dirt easily, and downright shocked as a flower springs from the hole as he pulls his finger out of it again. "How the heck does that work?" he says. "Maybe there was a seed down there," he guesses.

He glances at her, and then makes a fist and shoves it into the dirt up to his elbow. It's like mud to him, he thinks in wonder, giving easily. And when he pulls his arm out again a tree shoots out, about as tall as he is when standing. He falls on his butt, almost sitting on the cub. "Whoops, sorry--would you look at that!" Then he sways. Adanna barely manages to leap out of the way before he falls on his back, sound asleep, as if he's been switched off at the wall.

The cub hesitates, looking up at the tree for a long moment before cautiously belly crawling over to the sleeping boy. She sniffs him, and then sniffs the arm he created the tree with, patting it twice with a paw before leaping back in caution. The hand doesn't even move.

So she lies down where she's at, resting her muzzle on her paws and just... waits. It's not like she can move well enough to go anywhere, anyway.

★ ★ ★

Emily and Ditto stare at each other for a long, long moment before Emily lets out a breath. "Nope, nothing," she says. "You look exactly like me."

"But we were going to learn how to make me look like Trent!" Ditto says.

"I know, I know. But... why don't we go watch him and Max? That'll give us some ideas!" Emily stops as she sees the hesitant look on Ditto's face. "What?"

"Don't you think he's being too nice?" Ditto asks her. "It's not going to last. He'll probably realize we can't change me and then dump us for someone better--"

"We aren't dating him," Emily says. "I mean I'm not dating him. He's just going to be my partner--he can date anyone he likes."

"Like that new girl?" Ditto asks. "She's really pretty. Like really, really pretty--you saw how he reacted when she showed up!"

"Yeah," Emily says, sitting down and pouting slightly.

"And what about his parents... do you really think they love us?" Ditto asks. "We thought that Geoff and Marlina liked us, but look how that turned out."

"But they don't have to choose between us and Trent, right? And Trent promised and they backed him up and--and--" Emily lets out a pathetic sigh. "Maybe we should move into the dorms before they get tired of us."

"Yeah... if they get tired of us we'll probably die or something," Ditto says. "I mean, just one hit from Trent--"

"He won't hit us! He won't! Even if he gets tired of us, he'll not hit us," Emily says, looking down at her hands. "He made a promise on the Liberty name. It's important."

"Yeah, but either way we should move," Ditto says, "because they might like us now, but who can say if they'll like us later? Even Mr. Nico seemed to think we're troublemakers. Why else would he say we should prank people?"

"Because we slit those skirts," Emily points out quite logically.

"Oh, right," Ditto says, grinning as she remembers. "That was funny."

"See? We ARE troublemakers," Emily says. "But... I like being with them," she whispers, hugging her knees to her chest.

"Which is why we should be the ones to leave first," Ditto says. "Before Trent gets a girlfriend or Jeanie decides that--that we're not girly enough or something, or before Ken decides we're too much trouble or--"

Emily lets go of her legs and reaches for her doppelganger, hugging her tightly, and being hugged back. "Yeah," she says. "We'll--we'll talk to them after school."

The fight is brutal, even though we had been planning on making it quick. I pick up another slab of the metal field that we've torn up and twist, slinging it like a discus through the air. It gets caught in Max's gravity, floating for a moment before it starts to distort, rolling into a gigantic cone. Then, with an evil grin, he sends it slamming straight for me at an astonishing speed. It slams into my shoulder, tossing me back and ripping through the sleeve of my shirt to pin me to the exposed rocky ground. I growl, because that actually stung a bit, and reach over, grabbing the giant dart. I pull it out of the ground, getting to my feet and wadding it into a gigantic ball.

"I'm just going to get it again, you know," Max taunts. "You'll never hit--" I throw it with all of my strength in the middle of his taunting, hitting him straight on and sending him flying. He's past the edges of the field. Hey, think we'll get in trouble if he's out of the field in the sky?

He manages to stop before hitting the security shield. Good thing, too, because him getting fried on the first day would probably be a bad thing. Now he's heading back for me, the giant ball of metal slamming into the field next to me. I reach down as it creates a giant crater, tugging at a rather large piece of rock that's jutting out of the ground. It's closer than the metal ball. Before I manage to free it from the dirt, Max slams into me, sending us both backwards into the crater.

"You're messing up my hair," he complains as he punches me in the face.

"You're messing up my face," I drawl, although he isn't, really, before slamming my fist into his gut and sending him flying. I get to my feet and race for the rock I'd almost gotten out, only to grunt as gravity hits me hard. I find myself fighting the urge to fall to my knees.

"So this is your limit?" Max asks. I manage to look up at him, although my head feels like it weighs a million pounds. He's sweating, and breathing hard. I wonder if this much gravity is hard for him to pull off for long.

"I..." I grit out, clenching my jaw and forcing my leg to come up. It does, a mere inch off the ground. "Can... keep... going."

"I can make it heavier... maybe," he says. But something's happening. It's like the gravity lightens, only to get heavier again. I'm almost positive he's starting to lose it.

I move my foot forward, stepping towards the rock. It's like carrying a planet, I think as I try not to crumble. But I can do it--

The gravity stops so quickly that I find myself floating in the air because I was resisting so hard. For a moment my eyes widen as I realize that I'm flying--then I plummet to the ground, landing on my butt. I'm almost not surprised when Max falls to the ground, unconscious.

So that's how you beat him, I think, even as he regains consciousness again. He sits up quickly, looking a bit panicked. "What just happened?" he asks.

"We found your limit," I tell him.

"I--" he stops, looking stunned. "I didn't see that coming," he admits, falling onto his back. "So... you really can beat me already..."

"But you're getting stronger, too, right?" I say. "It's like your dad. He's a lot stronger than when he was a kid, I bet. Plus you weren't using any tools. I bet it'd be a lot heavier if you actually used something as a focus, right?" Really, as the guy that barely managed to stay upright just now, should I be mentioning these things?

"Yeah... yeah, maybe," he says, but his expression isn't saying the same. "I guess you won."

"Nah, it was a tie. I barely managed to get a step in. But I say we call it quits for the day," I say. I want to check up on Emily, okay? If I can move, that is. Not that I'm going to say I'm worried about Sunny--but I am. Max's logic about the whole "if Zoe's cute to me Sunny should be cute to girls" is repeating in my mind and I'm trying not to picture the two of them getting along perfectly. Thing is, if I like Sunny as much as I do and like Emily as much as I do, doesn't it make sense that they would like each other, too?

"Oh, right, don't want Sunny stealing your girl, huh?" Max says, amused. "So it's official, now, right? She's your girlfriend?"

"Er... well..." I say, feeling a bit sheepish. "Not exactly?"

He stares at me, deadpan in expression. "So you expect her to ignore Sunny when you haven't even asked her to go out with you," he sums up. "Are you a moron? Back when I was still chasing Zoe you were my biggest worry! I did everything I could to make sure she knew how I feel--I still do! But you! You've got this perfect little Liberty girl in the making and you haven't even--you're a moron."

"She's fourteen," I protest. "She's also going through a lot--I can't just force her into something--"

"So you just don't say anything at all--but claim her as your future partner, huh?" Max says. "That's way more serious than asking her out for ice cream. Even if she doesn't have a clue what it implies, she's going to figure it out sooner or later, you moron!" He seems stuck on that word, I think, and he's poking me in the forehead, even though he has to reach up for that.

"Okay, okay! I'll ask her out!"

"Ask who out?" I hear Emily and Ditto ask from behind me. They're several feet away from me and I figure they haven't been there that long, but they look worried.

"Um--" I say, forcing myself onto my feet. Man I'm sore. But that's not the important part. Do you have any clue how embarrassing it would be to be turned down in front of Max?

"We need to talk to you," Ditto says before I can figure out what to say. "In private," she adds.

She's letting Ditto talk for her again, I think a bit darkly. When Ditto does the talking it's a sure sign that Emily's thinking something she doesn't feel bold enough to say aloud.

"I'll just go check on Zoe," Max says, getting up and slapping me on the back of the head lightly before walking away. I watch him leave, wondering if I really want to have this conversation at school. What if she turns me down?

"Okay," I say, shoving my hands into my pockets. "What have you two decided?" They're the same girl, right? So why does it feel like they're going to be twice as much trouble? Probably because they will be, I admit, remembering the incident with the skirts, or the time they threatened to beat me up.

"We want to move into the dorms," Ditto announces.

"Why?" I ask.

"Because--because--"

"You'd be all alone," I say. "Mom would be heartbroken, Dad would be worried out of his mind, I would be--"

"Because we aren't a part of your family and you're going to get tired of us!" Emily bursts out.

"You really think that?" I ask.

"And you're already planning on asking someone out--and I don't want to be there while you date someone!" she finishes, her hands fisted at her sides.

"You sort of have to be there, though," I say, wondering why I feel so calm. A part of me is panicking, I think, but it's only a tiny part. Most of me is going, "So you're jealous?"

Wait, I just said that out loud.

"Of course we're--" Ditto starts out.

"Yes! I'm jealous!" Emily bursts out. Then she stops, looking shocked. She looks at Ditto, who's looking back at her, their expressions exactly the same. "I'm supposed to be your partner, but you just stared at the new girl--and I know she's pretty, okay? But she's a super villain and she doesn't like heroes and you won't get anywhere with her so you're just going to get turned down! And you'll deserve it! And I won't feel sorry for you!"

"Yeah, I stared at her," I admit. "Then I woke Sunny up, remember? Sunny wants a girlfriend, and seriously, who better for a plant grower than a panther shape shifter? They're both nature based! And I felt guilty because I wasn't going to let him have a chance at flirting with you."

"What?" they both ask.

"We had this whole argument over whether capes should date norms or not, but if I'm going to be a proper Liberty, well I'd prefer a cape as a partner... and as a girlfriend. But I was going to give him a chance at first. He's my best friend, you know? I owe him more than he'll ever guess. But then you! You two sit on my bed, grin at me, and tell me that you're going to beat me up if I mess up. I wanted to see it happen," I say honestly.

They're staring at me. "You're really weird," they say.

"Yeah, I know," I admit. "So I cheated. Claiming you as my future partner is absolutely cheating. See, I should have asked you out first."

They look at each other, she looks at herself--how exactly are you supposed to put that, anyway? Ditto poofs out of existence, leaving Emily standing in front of me, looking extremely vulnerable. "When you say partner..." she starts out slowly, "does it mean I should pick a name like Divine Justice like Mastermental said?"

"We'll get you a hammer," I say.

"Why a hammer?"

"Because it can be called the Hammer of Justice."

"Super heroes are weird, too," she says. She's not looking at me, she's looking down, and her face is bright red. "But--but if we're boyfriend and girlfriend and living in the same house--it's just... it doesn't seem right," she says, flushing again. "That's even more reason for me to move into the dorms and--"

"If it's that big of a problem you can move in with Aunt Liz," I say.

"What?"

"She's moving into the apartment next to ours anyway," I explain, shrugging. "It's not like it'll be so far that Mom worries or that you can't come over for dinner whenever you want, right? I mean we'd have to ask her, of course, but I doubt she'll mind. And Liz gets lonely," I add.

"She won't mind?"

"She's already told me she likes you a lot," I say honestly. "She thought that skirt thing you did was awesome. Then again, she was raised by Nico, so you kind of have to take her sense of humor with a grain of salt. But--I forgot. Will you be my girlfriend? No running away, no thinking I'm going to chase Cub, I mean, seriously, half the time there are two of you bugging me, I think I've got enough trouble on my plate--"

"You just admitted it!" she accuses me.

"Admitted what?"

"You called me trouble!"

"Em," I say patiently, "you ARE trouble."

"But you didn't have to admit it!" she says. "How would you like it if I called you hardheaded?"

"I am hardheaded," I say. I'm not about to deny that one, especially after that fight with Max.

"Or overbearing or heavy handed or a pain in the butt?"

"All of those things?" I ask, feeling a bit wounded.

"And a flirt!" she says, pointing at me. "That thing with the stairs and the foot and--and your dad walked in on us!" Which sounds really bad when she puts it that way, doesn't it? But it was perfectly innocent! You know, you saw it!

"There's nothing wrong with flirting with you!" I protest.

"You almost gave me a heart attack!" she accuses me. "You--you--Bossa Nova!"

"Think it's Casanova, actually," I offer, "and I'm absolutely not!" I hear the faintest of "poofs" behind me and turn just in time for Ditto to launch herself at me. While she's doing that Em jumps me from the other side, trying to dogpile me--and failing. What? I doubt she weighs a hundred pounds soaking wet.

"And how are you so comfortable with there being two of me?" Emily demands as they try and wrestle me down. It's not working very well. "You pervert!"

Even my ears turn red at this one. "I--I am not a pervert!"

"He's way too comfortable with two of us!" Ditto agrees. "He's thinking two girlfriends in one!"

"I'm thinking twice as much trouble to deal with is what I'm thinking!" I protest. "You're lucky that I'm so understanding and helpful!"

"He just called us trouble again!" Ditto complains, tugging on my ears.

"Man am I glad I'm a tank," I mutter as I hear someone laughing behind me. I turn, Emily and Ditto both hanging off of me, and look at practically the rest of the school just standing there, enjoying the show. "Is school over yet?" I say, shoving my hands in my pockets as the two try their hardest to wrestle me to the ground. They press their feet against my back and tug as hard as they can on my shoulders.

"Why. Won't. You. Fall?" they demand together.

"I'm pretty sure he already has," Mega says, shaking his head. "And yes, school is over for the day, we'll start the actual classes tomorrow."

"Where's Sunny?" I ask as one of the two hanging on me tries biting my neck--hard. "Hey, now, no biting!" I say, tugging at her.

"Take back the trouble comment," the other demands.

"Okay, fine. You are a sweet, understanding girlfriend that will cause no trouble whatsoever--now stop biting me!" She stops biting. "Where's Sunny?" I ask.

"Asleep behind the science building," Nico says as he joins the group. "I'll get him in a bit."

"Why?"

"I think growing the tree knocked it out of him."

"He grew a tree? Oh, wait, Adanna's not here either, is she?" Emily asks. "Where's she at?"

"She's stuck up the tree," Nico says, completely straight faced.

CHAPTER NINE

I wind up carrying Sunny home. Unfortunately Adanna shifted back to her human form and escaped the tree before we got to see what happened, but I'm positive that somehow Nico has it on tape somewhere. I really wish I could have seen it, I think as my best friend snores right next to my ear.

"So Nico's taking Adanna home, right?" Emily asks, her face still flushed. I think she's a bit embarrassed now that everyone (except Sunny, he never woke up) knows that we're dating. Not that we can really go out on a date with how things are, but you know what I mean.

"Yeah," I say.

"I should ask Liz about moving in," she says.

"Yeah. She'll say yes, though."

"But Jeanie won't mind, will she?"

"She might," I admit. "I think she likes having a daughter."

"But I'm not her daughter."

"You're close enough," I say. "Sunny, seriously, do you have to drool on my neck?" I complain as we get to the apartment building. Something makes me stop, glance around, and then up. Taurus is sitting on the roof of the building next to our apartments. Knowing that it's just him I let out a sigh of relief. "Wake up, man, we're home."

"Kitty," Sunny mutters against my neck before sliding off, stumbling to the panel and tapping his hand against it before going through the security.

"Kitty?" I ask Emily.

"Maybe he saw Adanna's panther form?" she offers. "I dunno."

We both head into the apartment building.

"So you two are finally officially dating, huh?" Dad asks as we step into the apartment. "It's about time! But we have some rules to lay down before we go any further--"

"Emily wants to move in with Liz," I say, heading for the couch to drop the sleeping Sunny down.

"What?" Mom asks. "And shouldn't you take Sunny to his room if he's going to sleep?"

"It's another floor, and I figure he can sleep through anything, so why bother?" I say as Emily comes in behind me. I head over to her, draping an arm over her shoulders.

"What's this about moving out?" Dad asks.

"It's um--well, if we're dating, don't you think it's too early to be living in the same house?" she says. "I mean, we just started dating and--I don't know. It seems like a really big step... even though we already were living together but we weren't dating so--"

"Oh, you're so adorable," Mom says, wrapping her arms around Emily in a hug. "I'll call Liz and we'll discuss it, okay? But you can come over whenever you need us, okay? You don't have to knock or anything, got it?"

"Yeah," Emily says, grinning widely. "Oh, but if Liz doesn't want to--"

The door opens and Liz steps in, looking excited. "I'll do it!" she says.

"You--wow you move fast," I say. "How long have you been eavesdropping anyway?"

"Since you came in," she says, crossing over to Emily to tug her out of Mom's arms. "I've always wanted to be a mother!" she says happily. "We'll go shopping for clothes together and train together and cook together--"

"Can't... breathe..." Emily gasps, looking a bit overwhelmed.

Liz loosens her hug, patting Emily's head fondly. "Sorry, sorry, I'll be more careful until you're older," she promises.

"So you don't mind?" Emily asks her.

"Mind? I'm excited!" Liz says. "It gets really boring living alone, you know, but Nico wouldn't let me move into his apartment, saying all his rooms were already taken. And this way you can come over here whenever I'm working late, so you won't get lonely, either."

I move over to Dad's side, leaning closer to whisper silently, "This is okay, right?"

"Liz practically lives with us whenever she's not working, anyway," he whispers back just as silently. "I think it'll be just fine."

"Good," I say, grinning. "So how am I going to take her out on a date when we're stuck in the apartment, anyway?" I ask, going straight to the problem.

"You'll come up with something," he says, messing up my hair with a grin.

★ ★ ★

Panther had invited Nico to stay for dinner, but Nico had to turn him down. And explaining to a super villain about another super villain hunting their children, he thinks as he pulls to a stop in front of the apartments, it hadn't been easy. *There are rules*, Panther had said so sharply that Nico felt guilty and he wasn't even the one doing it. Their children were supposed to be safe from the dangers of being capes. Their children were to be protected.

And they will be, Nico had sworn to his friend, *on my honor as the son of Superior himself,* although he felt no need to mention just how useless Superior had been to his own children. But now Nico is the father, and as the father he finds himself swearing such things because it carries the weight he needs it to.

His daughter is beautiful--a masterpiece of technopathy in the making, one that will have no limitations in the future. His son is a masterpiece as well, the complete opposite of his sister yet just as amazing. In just a few weeks, he thinks with amusement, he's fallen head over heels for the kids, willing to take on the entire super world for them.

And one of that world is sitting on the roof of the apartment right next to his.

"Taurus," he says, landing on the rooftop next to the large Minotaur man. "I think they're safe now."

"Technico," Taurus says, looking up at him, "how can we trust you?"

The question shouldn't have been as surprising as it is, Nico thinks as he looks the huge Minotaur in the eyes. Idly he reaches into his back pocket (yes, flying while in civvies--but he used the mask, he thinks, that should count for something) and pulls out his wallet.

"Are you trying to bribe me?" Taurus asks.

Nico pulls out a small circular disk, tossing it down onto the roof and hitting it with his power. The disk starts to spin, bringing up a hologram between the two of them. "Hey Dad!" the image of Zoe says. "You forgot to eat again, didn't you? What do you want? I'm only going to ask once, and if you don't reply I'm making you a bowl of cereal, got it?" The image changes, and Sunny stands there where Zoe was. "Hey, Dad, would you STOP putting flowers next to my bed at night? Sheesh, I know Jeanie asked you to, but they keep trying to crawl into bed with me!"

The recording stops and he leans down to grab the disk again. "I made this," he says, holding it between two fingers, "in case they stick me back in the Cells. If I go, this is the only way I'll ever be able to see them again. Knowing that," he goes on, "do you really think I'm going to risk it?"

"I see," Taurus says quietly. "Do they know about that?"

"No, Zoe would want to know how it works and explode it," Nico says, grinning slightly for a second before going serious again. "This game we play, usually both sides follow the unspoken rules. Even Pan was outraged at the idea of our children being hunted, did you know that? But my... brother, and his partner, they're not playing by the rules. And when it brings my kids into play--well, if I need to, neither will I. So I'm going to return that question, Taurus, and add a bit of weight to it. Those two are the most important things I have in this world. How can *I* trust *you* to keep them safe?"

"It's easy enough," Taurus says, shifting into his human form and smiling slightly. "You can trust me because I'm pretty sure I'm in love with your little sister."

"What?"

"Ever since the day I met her fifteen or so years ago, right after you were tossed into the cells and she was brought to the hall. I was eighteen at the time, she was fifteen or sixteen. She looks at me, this gawky, skinny black kid that's only starting to grow into his shifting, and dismisses me completely."

"Why?"

"Because it's really hard to live up to you." He laughs. "I thought I was long over that, too," he admits. "I mean, sure, I followed all her jobs, kept a tape of the Hero TV reports and interviews... called it being a fanboy. There's no one out there like her, Technico. Thing is," he says, "I'm not a kid anymore. I'm an A class hero, even without flight, your computer said so itself. I'd like to think this time around it won't be that easy to dismiss me without hearing me out."

"So you think you can impress Liz?" Nico asks, grinning slightly. "You know, you might just manage--MIGHT. She's hard to handle even on her good days, though."

"I'm willing to work for it. I think having you accept it will give me a bit of a boost, not going to lie," he says.

Nico looks at him, thinking about everything he's seen on the man in front of him. Taurus is, as Trent put it, a cape that even America's Son admires. He's straight forward, hard working, and most importantly when it came to capes, close to sane. "I think," Nico says finally, "I won't mind. But Liz is a full grown woman, you know. She'll make her own decisions. And since you're being so honest, I will be too. You and the others, I expect you to keep me from having to do something that will get me tossed back into the cells. Do you get what I mean?"

"We'll stop them," Taurus says. "We'll put them in the cells."

"I'm not sure they'll hold them."

"Then we'll deal with that when it comes to it," Taurus says, "as a group. I'm going to keep you out of the cells, as long as you're willing to do what you're doing. More kids will come, you know."

"Double M's got his eyes on one already."

"More than just the ones Double M grabs," Taurus says. "I only wish I'd had a thing like this when I was a kid." He stands, stretching for a second before saying, "I'll get going, then," and jumping off the roof to land lightly on the concrete street below.

He's gone the next second, leaving Nico standing on the roof alone.

Almost hesitantly he pulls out his wallet again, opening it and pulling out a disk much like the first one but older. He stares at it, flipping it between his fingers in a manner that says he has done this many times before, and then he throws it to the ground, hitting it with his power.

"Nico," the hologram of the beautiful woman says. She has thick red hair that cascades over her shoulders and eyes so green they outdo emeralds. She's wearing a colorful broomstick skirt and peasant top. "I love you, Nico." Her hand reaches out, a ghost of a touch on his shoulder. "I love you."

"And the earth shot up and there were flowers all around him!" the man says enthusiastically as he follows Star around her lab. "It was amazing! That's why more people need powers, right? That way they can sleep wherever they go without needing a bed-- I'm really tired of that cot, you know--"

"That's ni--" Star stops, putting down the slide she was about to put into the microscope. "Honey?" she asks, turning to him. "Would you repeat what you just said?"

"I'm really tired of the cot?"

"No, before that."

"That way you can sleep--"

"No, it was something about the earth. What happened with the earth?" she asks in a very patient tone.

"Oh, the sleeping boy--it helped him!" he says. "It just shot up under him and made a bed, all on its own. It was really cool."

"And the flowers?"

"They grew up all around him," he says. "Didn't you hear me the first time? You weren't listening, were you," he accuses her.

"Oh, I'm listening very, very carefully right now."

"Okay."

"So this boy, do you know who he is?"

"Um... he looked a lot like that man's daughter--the one that isn't my daughter. Maybe it's her brother?"

"I see," she says. "So he's... an elementalist Superior. I see." She turns back to the lab counter, picking up the slide. "Honey, why don't you go read your comics for a bit. It sounds like you had a very busy day. You need a break."

"Sure, that sounds good," he says, turning and starting out the door again. Idly he reaches into his pocket, digging through all the strange things he'd found that day. He pulls out a seed, looking at it curiously as he walks down the hall.

Something makes him stop next to one of the glassed in cells, and his eyes fall on the red haired woman laying sound asleep inside. Absently he reaches up, touching the pad that makes the glass wall slide open, and goes in.

"Hi," he says, moving to her bedside. "I brought you something." He holds up the seed, looking at it with a slight smile, and then reaches down for her hand, tucking it into the palm. "Sleep well," he says softly before walking out of the room. The glass slides shut behind him. No one sees the hand holding the seed tighten into a fist.

Next Cape High:

CAPE HIGH
BOOK THREE: HELLO KITTY

I am Adanna Francesca Panterus, I am the fifteenth generation of the Panther family, daughter of the present Panther, Chinaza Michael Panterus and his wife, Amara Panterus.

Mama was a famous model up until about four years ago. She quit when she got pregnant with my little brother, Kayode Michael Panterus, AKA Cub or Cubby. I'm just going to put this out right now, because it's one of those issues I keep running into when I meet people. Papa is always making me take my hat off and show off my face because he thinks I look like Mom, but really, I don't see it. I mean, Mama's gorgeous. She's in her forties, but she's still so beautiful that whenever we go into public all the norms, especially the men, stare at her as she goes past, but she ignores them. I mean, not only is she beautiful she's married to the most amazing man in the world, so why would she bother with norms?

Papa's a super villain. But he's way more than just that--he's a world renowned scientist and he's gotten all sorts of awards for his discoveries in biological studies. He specializes in animal genetics, which makes sense, considering our family's powers. We're shape shifters.

Mama's not, of course. Mama's an animal speaker, but she can't shift. She's never really done much with her abilities, honestly, other than take care of the big cat sanctuary we run.

But I guess you're probably wondering why I'm stuck up this tree, huh? Yeah, I was trying to ignore that fact, but it's pretty obvious when you look down... way down... far, far, faaaar down. I feel a little dizzy, actually. The world seems to sway in front of my eyes and I dig my claws into the bark of the tree, not wanting to fall off--yes, I said claws. I'm shifted at the moment, and I can't turn back because it's part of self study, thanks to the principal of Cape High.

143

"How did you get up there again?" I hear someone say from below.

"Leave her," Taurus says mildly. "She's going to learn how to get out of trees sooner or later." Taurus is a super hero. That's irritating enough, as far as I'm concerned, but it gets worse. His shape shifted form? It's amazing. It's this massively huge minotaur, one three times larger than his human form. My shape shifted form? It's a tiny little runt of a panther cub. Needless to say I'm not very happy being cubsat by him--so I ignore him completely.

It's Sunny that I look at. He's holding up his hands, offering to catch me. "C'mon," he says in a sweet, coaxing voice. "It's okay, I'll catch you." Sunny is 1) Lazy, 2) extremely powerful, 3) growing more powerful as the day goes by, and 4) a hero in training. Yes. This short little guy with big green eyes that falls asleep at the drop of a hat is everything I can't stand--especially when I'm stuck up a tree again!

"Shouldn't you be napping right now?" Taurus asks.

"I woke up," Sunny says, grinning. Yes, he actually naps for self study. How useless is that? I don't see why all the adults are so awed over him. Sure he's got some interesting powers over plants and dirt and whatever, but as a super in training he's shameless and--I let out a hiss as the tree branch moves lower on its own, literally reaching for the boy that I hate the most. "There we go," Sunny says, gently prying me from the limb. "That's better."

He's holding me right in front of his face, so I do the first thing I can think of. I bop him on the nose with a paw--wait, there were supposed to be claws there. Why are my claws not working? Stupid kitten form! "Rowr," I say, which is not nearly as impressive as I'd planned it to be, either.

He laughs. "Look at that face!" he says. "You look like I've ruined Christmas!"

Taurus takes me out of his hands. "Enough teasing her," he says. "Go check on your sister or help Emily with her studies," he adds, putting me on the ground. I start forward, but I still haven't gotten used to the four legs and a tail thing, so I promptly fall on my face. "And no laughing," Taurus warns.

"She's just--it's just--" Sunny starts out. I can almost finish the sentence, I think, "She's just so clumsy, she's just so funny looking," or something like that, I think as I lay down, sulking.

"Go on," Taurus says, pushing Sunny off. He waits until the boy is gone before coming over and sitting down next to me. "I got you something," he says, pulling out his smartphone from his pocket and putting it in front of me. He brings up a video then pushes play before I get the chance to figure out how to back away. A leopard appears on the screen. "This is an African Leopard," he says. "Like you. Watch how it moves for a while."

I find myself staring, watching closely as the leopard pads across the screen, focusing on the muscle movements, the way the tail moves. I've seen big cats move, we've got them out back, but the body shape of the leopard is different. The legs are shorter and the body longer--

"When I started shifting," Taurus says, "I turned into a calf. I was about your age. And if you think being a cub is awkward, try having four long and extremely skinny legs and a huge body. I tripped over everything, especially myself. Your father," he goes on, "has three forms. I've seen them--I have them on this, we'll be watching it later. He's got the normal sized panther, the gigantic panther, and the were-panther. I'm betting you'll grow up to have all those, yourself. But it takes time and hard work."

I look at him, tail flicking once, then back at the video. He lets out a laugh. "He's right, you're extremely expressive in this form," he says. "I know... of them all, Sunny's probably the most annoying, isn't he? He's only a little older than you, but he's catching onto his powers so fast--like the tree branch? That must have really made you irritated, didn't it?"

Yes. Yes it absolutely had. He doesn't even have to work to overcome problems like the ones I face--and he never DOES work! All he does is nap in the sun or sun bathe or be lazy--which really, aren't all of those being lazy? And the worst part? The tree I keep climbing up when startled is all his fault to begin with! And the fact that I was startled is all Taurus's fault, so really, why am I sitting here agreeing with him? I look at Taurus darkly.

"Okay, okay, you don't like me much, either, I get that," he says, laughing again. "But listen, I went through exactly what you're going through right now--hero, villain, all shape shifters have similar experiences. And I wouldn't tell just anyone this, but Cub, you're probably the closest that the shape shifters get to a princess, no matter what side we're on."

I look at him, startled, but he looks sincere. "As far as I know, you're the first shape shifter of this generation. We all expect big things from you, especially with your background and training. That you have a little brother, that you've lost the official title of Cub, well that's just tradition being ugly. Nowadays we watch our female supers with as much anticipation as we do our males, you know. More, in some cases. Remember when your dad found out that Zoe takes after Technico and Sunny doesn't?"

I nod slightly, and he goes on, "Your own father knows that she's the one to watch when it comes to becoming a super villain. Sunny, well, Sunny's in a different line of work than the rest of us," he admits. "Or he will be, if he follows what his mother was doing."

"Rowr?" I hear myself say. So I'm curious! It isn't a sin to be curious! Although I really do hate that "curiosity killed the cat" line, so please don't bring it up.

"Sunny will go on a mission to save the rainforest, or something along those lines," Taurus says. "He'll be involved in the environmental issues, and it's only right that he is. So technically he'll carry the title 'hero,' but... well, you'll never have to go up against him. If you were to become a hero, you might work beside him once in a while, if you're lucky. But the way you're going now, you'll never have to deal with him again after you graduate. Although," he says, "you might if you continue with the endangered animal work that your Dad keeps hidden."

I'm so startled that I shift into my human form, staring at him. "Don't tell people of our work with animals!" I say, hissing still. "It's... personal business, not villain business! I don't know how you found out--"

"Adanna," he says, "we all know. We just don't say anything because it doesn't work with the whole heroes and villains stuff.

Your dad puts on quite the show as a super villain, extremely flashy. I'm pretty sure he's got a massive fan-following."

"He is a proper super villain and highly admired for his abilities!" I say heatedly.

"And has an extremely beautiful wife," he says in a teasing tone.

"Yes! He does! My mother is gorgeous!" I say, falling back and staring at the sky. "I'm supposed to be in cat form longer, aren't I?" I add in a mumble, not looking forward to it.

"Another twenty minutes," he says, looking at his watch.

I sigh, and shift back, just lying on my back in cub form for a moment, my paws in the air. Then I twist, rolling to my feet and start walking that same, awkward walk as before. Right paw, back paw, left paw--trip.

"Relax," Taurus says. "Stop thinking so much, you're going to trip yourself up. Get used to the skin you're in, cub, it's still you, when you think about it." I try bringing my tail up, like the cat's in the video--and a feather touches my nose. I pull back, sneezing, then look up the string tied to the feather, expecting Taurus.

"Hi," Emily says. No, I think, sniffing, that's not Emily, it's Ditto. And she thinks I want to play with a cat toy.

"Rowr," I say, giving her as dirty a look as I can manage in cat form.

"It'll help!" she says, bopping me with the feather again. I swat it, trying to get it out of my face.

"Emily, is there a reason you're here?" Taurus asks.

"Oh, Nico says he wants to talk to Cub," she says, dangling the feather in my face again. "So he sent me!"

"Oh, really."

"Well he caught me spying, so he said I should make myself useful--I think she likes the cat toy," she says, making me look up guiltily from where I've started batting the feather back and forth. I ah--okay, it's more entertaining than falling on my face all the time, I admit it. "I've got more!" she says, digging another cat toy out of her pocket.

147

I shift to human form, sitting on my knees in front of the petite redhead--and promptly sneeze again because the feather is on my nose. "I don't need cat toys," I say. Although, actually, it had been sort of fun--but Emily (or her doppelganger in this case) is not only a hero in training, she is a hero's partner in training, and definitely not someone I should be playing with. "Technico is in the science building?" I ask, getting to my feet and discreetly trying to dust my clothes off.

"Yep, he's watching everyone on his computer again," she says, putting her cat toys away. Does Emily create everything in Ditto's pockets as well? I wonder how I can ask without seeming too interested-- "I'll take you!" she says, grabbing my hand and tugging.

"You're a super hero," I say. "You shouldn't be grabbing a super villain's hand so willingly!"

She looks up at me, a hurt expression on her face that makes me feel as guilty as if I'd kicked a kitten. Slowly she lets go of my hand. "Yeah, I guess," she says, her shoulders falling as she shoves her hands in her jean pockets. "I'm sorry."

"Adanna," Taurus says from behind. "Why don't you go on, you know where it is."

I nod, not looking at Emily as I go past her, heading for the front of the building we're behind to go see Technico. Why do these people not understand the lines between heroes and villains? It drives me crazy sometimes! I'm not supposed to be friends with super heroes, I'm here to learn how to defeat them! But one after the other--especially Emily and Sunny--they come and bother me while I'm trying to do my self study!

And Emily is so adorable, I think, irritated with my weakness for cute little things. I feel so guilty right now, okay? But she needs to learn this lesson before she winds up getting hurt, I tell myself firmly. Some wicked super villain will someday use that curious nature against her and--

And her massive partner will show up, save her, and take out the entire building along the way, I think dryly as I hear the sounds of fighting in the distance. Her boyfriend is NOT adorable. Her boyfriend is a tank--one of those supers that are impossible to deal with because they have few weaknesses and tend to be very by-the-book, as my Papa has told me. I feel no guilt whatsoever about not being nice to Trent Styles. One day I'm sure I'll run up against him. I really, really hope that I've got my shape shifting perfected at that time, though.

"You called," I say as I take the final step up the stairs to the second floor of the science building. Nico's pretty much claimed it for himself, although it's supposed to be a lab for mad science experiments. There are all sorts of mechanical parts scattered on the long desks meant for students, and he's in the middle of welding something together with his fingertip--that's something I didn't know he could do.

"Yeah, come here, Cub," he says, motioning to me.

"I am no longer called Cub," I say, feeling a bit irritated with how people keep calling me that here.

"I know, I know, but your little brother isn't here right now, so come on," he says. He holds up a helmet, as if I'm supposed to know what it's for. "I want to try something."

"And it has something to do with me?" I ask, looking at the helmet instead of him. Of all the people in this school, Technico is the one I've been told I can trust the most. He's an old friend of my Papa's. But honestly, he's rather strange. I don't know if you've heard this theory before, but the stronger a super is, the stranger they tend to be mentally. Oh, they can be geniuses, just look at Nico or my Papa, but that doesn't mean their hobbies are all understandable--or even explainable.

"It won't hurt," he says. "I just want to see if it works."

I look at him, knowing what he's not saying. "Papa told me that you might try and experiment on me," I tell him. "But you have your own children to experiment on, so--"

"Wouldn't work," he admits. "Zoe would take it over and Sunny would fall asleep."

"I see, then perhaps--"

"Emily's a telepath, so it's sort of pointless considering she'll learn to do things on her own, and Trent and Max need all the sparring training they can get. You're the only one in the group that fits the bill. Now sit here," he says, pulling out a chair. I head for it reluctantly, sitting down and watching him closely. He slips the helmet over my head. I can't see anything, it's completely dark. "Now I want you to picture a tree."

I close my eyes, picturing the tree from behind the building, since I just came from there. I instantly picture myself up on the branch again, staring down at the ground.

"Are your eyes open?" he asks.

"No."

"Open them."

I open my eyes, jerking as I realize I'm staring down at the ground from the tree limb. "Good," I hear Nico say. "So it does work. This will help me with the kid when I get it finished." He takes the helmet off of me and I blink at him. "Possibly."

"Is that to read people's minds?" I ask.

"There's a boy not much older than you that's stuck in a coma," he says. "If I can read his mind I'll be able to find out where they did what they did to him."

"But isn't Mastermental--"

"The metal interferes with his powers," Nico says. "This is reading electrical waves, so hopefully I can adjust for the metal that's lacing his brain. It's worth a try, at least. Now," he says, dropping down in the chair next to me. "I've been watching your training."

"I... see," I say, looking down. So he's been watching all my awkward falls and pathetic attempts? I--

"I think Emily had a good idea," he says.

"What?" I yelp.

"Cat toys look like a perfect way to go," he says. "I've been thinking about it for a while, actually. You need to enjoy your training at this stage, Cub. Playing is how cats learn to hunt, right? But I don't think you like anyone enough to let them see you play, do you?" he says, almost to himself.

"It--it isn't that I dislike them," I say a bit awkwardly. "All," I have to add when he just looks at me.

"So what if we build you something you can use?" he asks. "Like those towers that housecats have. Towers to climb, holes to climb into, feathers everywhere--what do you think?" he asks.

"I'm not a cat!" I protest. "I'm a super villain!"

"But you're a super villain that turns into a cat," he says. "I think the problem is that you're so focused on being a villain that you don't feel able to relax here. Yes, we're surrounded by super heroes. I know it can be intimidating, but if they were going to hurt you, do you really think I'd let them anywhere near you?" he asks, looking me straight in the eye. "Your dad is one of my oldest friends, Cub. That makes you extremely important to me. Sort of like a niece, I guess."

I feel a hint of a flush cross my face and look down. I have met some of my Papa's friends before, but I've never met one that so blatantly says something like that. "I will... try," I say. "It might take me a while, I don't know why it's so hard to move in that form, but I won't give up."

"Good girl," he says. "And I know Sunny annoys you, but you can't really blame the kid--"

"I absolutely can!" I protest. "He's constantly showing up to bother me--you need to change his morning study, he does *not* sleep long enough!" He's laughing now, I notice.

"Because there's this cute little kitty just around the building," he says. "And if he times it right he'll get to see her cat form."

I scowl, crossing my arms over my chest. "I realize that the cat form is ridiculous," I say, "but that gives him no right to come and laugh at me!"

"You're right, you're right," he says all too easily. "He has absolutely no right to laugh at your cub form."

"Tell him that!"

"I don't think that's what he's laughing at, actually," he says. "But fine, I'll tell him to quit because you're so self conscious about it. Now, I think we've wasted enough time that you won't have to transform again. So you can go."

"I--thank you," I say, feeling pathetic at being seen through so easily.

"I'll have a playground built by tomorrow," he says. "But you might try being nicer to Emily, you know. She came up with the idea that might get you moving easier."

I nod as I leave the room.

~About the Author~

R.J. Ross has been writing since junior high, when she discovered that it could help her keep an A in English Class. She lives in Missouri, where she works as a secretary for the family business and spends all of her free time writing. If you would like to see more of her work, you can find several short stories at amazon.com/author/rjross!

Like her on Facebook for bonus material such as character profiles, unpublished information, and status updates at https://www.facebook.com/capehigh! Or check out her blog for free Cape High short stories at https://capehigh.wordpress.com or follow her on twitter @rjrosscapehigh

~~~~~~

~About the Cover Designer~

Cheyanne is a native Texan with a fear of cold weather and a coffee addiction that probably needs an intervention. She loves books, sarcasm, nail polish and paid holidays. She lives near the beach with her family, one spoiled rotten puppy and a cat that is plotting to take over the world, one scratched up welcome mat at a time.

A recent day-job quitter, Cheyanne can be found furiously typing on her computer, probably complaining on Twitter about how she should be writing. When she's not honing her procrastination skills, she's writing books for teenagers. She is the author of several books for teens and recently turned her love of superheroes and writing for teens into books about teenage superheroes. Find more about her books at www.CheyanneYoung.com or follow her on Twitter @NormalChey

Made in the USA
Lexington, KY
03 November 2018